Fox

Sasha Avice

ISBN EBOOK: 978-0-6452714-0-9

ISBN PAPERBACK: 978-0-6452714-1-6

Cover by: ashwood designs

Newsletter

Subscribe to my newsletter via sashaavice.com for regular updates on WIPs, new releases, and thoughts on writing.

You'll receive two free novellas upon sign up.

Just want the books? No dramas: hit unsubscribe after you've downloaded them.

1

♥

FOX ROLLED OVER. THE light from the open window was streaming orange. He groaned and rubbed his eyes as he pushed himself up and swung his legs over the bed. He felt dizzy. He breathed in and it sounded wet. He shook it off and went for the bathroom.

No one else was up yet.

The hot water loosened up his chest. Fox couldn't tell if it was from smoking too much or he was actually getting sick. He got out and rubbed himself dry, tightened the towel around his waist and went back to his room. He pulled on boxers, yesterday's jeans and a clean shirt. He sat down, yanked on his boots, laced them and went for his cigarettes. He lit one and pocketed the packet, grabbed his wallet, and went out to get coffee.

She was up. She looked at him over the boiling kettle but said nothing.

"Hey," he said. His voice was gruff. He must be getting sick.

"Where're you going?"

And why did she always ask this? He glanced at the clock. Kalum would be here now, like he was every day, and they would go and do what they always did.

"Out."

Fox reached up for a travel mug. He had to turn his back to her to do it, and the position always made him uneasy. In theory, he could take her with a single hit, but in practice, he'd never do that and they both knew it.

"'Out' he says." She took a drag of her cigarette and the kettle pinged.

Fox balanced his cigarette between his lips, got two teaspoons of coffee and one sugar in his mug, aware of her beside him, and then reached for the kettle while trying to avoid eye contact.

He heard her drag, the paper crinkling as it burnt. He poured the water. He knew she was going to ask. It was Wednesday, she always asked.

"Got your pay yet?"

And there it was. He focused on screwing the lid on his mug, crushing his cigarette in her ashtray and keeping his breaths even. He felt her watching him and reading everything she needed to know in his movements.

"Just like your fucking father," she said. He could feel her gearing up to really let him have it when Austin rounded the corner, his gait purposeful as he went straight to the cupboard with the mugs.

"Hey."

"Hey," Fox replied and grabbed his mug. Fox didn't need to see her to know she'd shut up now.

"You need the car today?" she said to Austin.

"Nope," he replied and made his coffee.

"Catch ya," Fox said to the room, to Austin. He kept his eyes down and went for the door without looking back. He heard her sigh, but she didn't say anything else.

"Bye," Austin said, and Fox heard him heading back to his room, feet padding on the carpet.

Fox powered up the steep driveway and felt his chest wheeze with the effort.

Kalum was waiting at the top of their little hill. He had the window down, elbow out, and he was grinning like a madman. Fox tried to shake off the anxiety of the house and focus on the day ahead.

"Hey," he said to Kalum as he rounded the bonnet and went for the passenger seat.

"Yo," Kalum replied, still grinning.

"What're you smiling about?"

Kalum started the engine as Fox got in. He made the turn in the cul-de-sac and slowly dragged the car up the hill. Fox often felt like the car would roll right back down and go crashing through the kitchen window and flatten his mum where she stood brooding and sipping her coffee.

"Oh, nothing, just saw Clarissa coming back in."

Fox felt a flutter of worry. He buried it and focused on what else he thought about that – good for her.

"Good for her."

They were belting down the side road now, headed for the city.

"I dunno, she looked pretty wasted. Not wasted enough to not give me the finger, but you know."

Fox did know. He'd been on the receiving end of that finger his whole life.

He shrugged and looked out the window at the escarpment whipping by. "She's always gonna do what she wants."

Unlike me, he thought and wished, not for the first time, he had an ounce of his sister's courage.

"Carl said Tony said something about a new guy comin round later," Kalum said as they gunned it through the bushland at the base of the hill.

Fox shrugged again, what else could he do? Another new guy. More of the same. He'd be a racist, homophobic, sexist piece of shit like the rest of them. A terrified little boy pretending to be a man, Clarissa would say.

"Reckon he might pair him up with you to do runs."

That got Fox's attention.

"Why?"

Kalum slowed for the red light.

"Reckons we gotta go with someone older. Said it's too easy to roll us together."

The light turned green and they were off, the trees thinning as they got closer to the industrial area.

That's not what Tony would've said. He would've said it was too easy to roll a couple of fags together. Fox could see it. Kalum would've taken it with a grin but Fox would've seen the strain. Kalum would've been scared. Hurt. Even though Kalum was the straightest guy you'd ever meet. His embarrassing obsession with Clarissa, the way he could barely speak when a woman spoke to him, all tongue tied and trying not to look at their breasts; even the skimpies, who were clearly topless for a reason, Kalum, come on, Fox would say. Point was, he'd be taking it up the ass when hell froze over. Fox watched it crush him every time. He felt crushed by proxy.

"What's his name?"

"Tys? Ty? Somethin like that. He's Tony's cousin."

Fox screwed his face up. Kalum looked over and laughed. "I know, man."

The day kept getting better and better. If Carl was an asshole, Tony was the biggest fucking prick Fox had ever met. Austin asked why he hung out with these assholes. Fox always shrugged and said what else was he gonna do. It was where Kalum went, so he went. Austin gave him a look like he was stupid. Austin met Tony once when he picked Fox up and turned around and walked straight back to the car. Austin wouldn't even want to breathe the same air as that guy. Fox didn't either, but again, what else was he gonna do.

They turned onto the main road, but Kalum took a quick right for the side road, dragging the trip out. There were no trees now. Overgrown weeds and old warehouses. It was still early enough when they parked that Fox thought what he always did when the sun was still lurking at the top of the hills – the day hasn't gone to shit yet.

He took a deep breath and his chest rattled and Kalum asked if he still had that cough. Fox shook his head and undid his seatbelt.

Kalum cut the engine, but left the key turned enough that the music still played. It was some amped up eighties shit. They both hated it, but what were they gonna do? Buy a CD player? Fox could barely afford his cigarettes, and that was before his mum pilfered his pay each week.

"You know, we could just go," Kalum said.

Fox looked at him. Kalum was looking straight ahead at the warehouse. It was unremarkable. Could've been a place where work happened, could've been abandoned. It was neither.

"Go where."

Fox coughed after he said it; he settled the phlegm, hacked it up, then swallowed it down.

Kalum waited him out.

"I dunno, somewhere not here."

"Yeah? And how we gonna pay for the fuel?"

"Fuck, man, I dunno."

Fox lit another cigarette and tilted the open packet to Kalum.

"You pussies comin in or are ya just gonna sit here all day?"

Tony's gruff voice cut through their bubble in the car. Fox didn't even hear the fat fucker come up. Kalum fumbled the cigarette.

"Yeah, we're comin, we're comin," Kalum said as he bent down and scrambled around the floor under the wheel for the smoke.

"Well hurry the fuck up then, got a job for ya."

Tony walked up the asphalt and unlocked the door.

"Where's his bike?"

Fox thought that was a bloody good question. The fat fuck shouldn't be able to get the jump on them. He craned his head back. The street was empty except for an old Corolla about to make a U-turn. Candy. Not her real name. She caught Fox's eye and gave him a smile and a wave. Candy was nice but she made Fox uncomfortable. He nodded back anyway and glanced up to where Tony had disappeared inside the building.

Kalum lit the cigarette and turned the key. The music cut out and the sound of the street filtered in. The distant hum of traffic and then the sound of nothing, not even a bird.

2

♥

THE JOB WAS CLEANING and scrubbing the absolute shit-hole that was the bar and party area of the clubhouse. There'd been some bullshit here the night before and the place was disgusting. Fox picked up a can and a used condom was stuck to it.

"Fuck, really?"

Kalum looked over his shoulder and cracked up laughing.

"No, really. What the fuck is that doing out here?"

Kalum shushed him and hissed, "Ya know, they take Viagra and shit."

Fox scrunched his face up. And they fucked out here?

"You girls nearly finished in here?" Tony's voice came from behind them and Fox flinched.

Fox wanted to say, fuck off, of course we haven't, we only started on this dump an hour ago, but he said nothing and kept his eyes on Kalum.

The door opened and a flash of light cut through the space as somebody walked in. Fox couldn't make out who it was against the glare of morning sun other than male and tall, built.

"Taylor," Tony greeted.

Fox watched the guy, it must've been the cousin, walk over to Tony. His gait was loose if a little hunched. He was blinking his eyes like he was adjusting them. He looked like he was waking up or maybe he was just that relaxed. He shook Tony's hand.

"Hey, man," he said. His voice was deep but soft. Fox felt it rumble through him and felt embarrassed for noticing it.

Taylor glanced over Tony's shoulder and met Fox's eyes. Fox looked back, startled. He dropped his gaze to the condom and can in his hand and cringed before pitching it towards the bin. He missed and the sound clattered on the concrete as the can skipped past the bar.

Tony was saying something about "this pair of pussies" and Fox stopped listening. He was very focused on his steps as he went over to that godforsaken can, picked it up, brought his arm up above his head and hurled it into the bin.

"Fox'll be riding shotgun with you tonight."

Fox looked up at his name.

"Huh?"

He saw Taylor watching him. His expression was cold, but there was a focus in it that made Fox's skin prickle with nerves.

Fox skittered his eyes away and looked at Tony instead. He hated looking at Tony, he couldn't maintain eye contact, but for once it was the better option.

"Doin the laundry run, kid. Fucken keep up."

Fox shook his head. "I gotta shift."

Tony gave him a look like he was insane. And maybe he was. He usually had a shift, yeah, but he and Kalum made it work so he'd never had to mention it.

Before he could backtrack, Taylor spoke, "What time do you finish?"

"Uh, midnight?"

"Are you sure?" Taylor said and Fox swore he heard a smirk in it, but Taylor's face didn't change.

"I can bring Fox back down," Kalum piped up.

"You'll be with me and Carl," Tony said to him, then to Fox, "What's this fucking shift business?"

Fox opened his mouth, but Taylor spoke first, "I'll pick you up. Whereabouts?"

"The Kala," Fox replied, automatic.

Taylor nodded and turned back to Tony. "You wanna go over the runs with me?"

Tony narrowed his eyes at Fox but answered Taylor, "Yeah, come on."

Taylor met Fox's eyes as he followed Tony into the office. His face was still expressionless, but Fox swore there was a hint of a smile in his eyes as he went by. Fox quickly looked down again.

The door to the office closed behind them and Fox took a deep breath. The air caught his chest funny and he coughed, then he really coughed.

"Shit, man," Kalum was saying. He appeared by his side with a bottle of water.

Fox took it and waited until his cough had petered out to wet hacks and gasps of air. Then he took careful sips.

"You gonna be alright?" Kalum asked as Fox straightened.

Fox heaved a breath into his lungs. He gave a deep grunt to lift all the mucous and then nodded. He took another drink. He knew Kalum wanted to say more: You shouldn't be working. You shouldn't be doing a dish pig shift after this so your bitch of a mum can steal your pay. You shouldn't be doing drug runs all night after that. But he didn't. He wouldn't. They didn't talk like that.

"I'll be fine."

Fox capped the water and went back to picking up rubbish. Kalum muttered something but Fox wasn't listening. He was trying very hard not to think about how Taylor looked to him. He was wondering how he could sneak a few beers from the bar staff before Taylor picked him up so he'd be cool.

Before Taylor picked him up.

God. He was going to be in a car with him all night. He might need a six-pack.

3

F OX FINISHED UP THE last of the dishes, the heat and steam from
the kitchen doing wonders for his chest. He glanced at the clock.
Quarter to twelve. He'd managed to wheedle a beer out of Madison
in the front bar, but "Only one." Fox wiped his hands on the damp
towel, threw it over his shoulder and went and got the beer out of the
fridge. It'd have to be enough. At least it was a longneck. He figured if
he sculled it, he'd get enough of a buzz to be normal when Taylor got
here.

He cracked the beer and Madison poked her head in. "Some guy's
here for you?"

She said it in that snobby way that meant she was as impressed by
the physical manliness of Taylor as Fox was but wouldn't in a million
years deign to be attracted to a guy like that. Neither would Fox, but
for a billion other reasons, and a single pretty obvious one. Taylor was
a guy.

But, shit. Taylor was here.

Fox took a sip, then another, and then a big swig. Madison frowned
at him and then went out. Fox tossed the towel on the empty sink and
went to the back to get his hoodie. He was sweaty, but he knew the
evening chill would take care of it. He pulled his deodorant out of

his bag and gave himself a quick spray, ran his hand through his hair, and then pulled on his jumper. It'd have to do. He finished his beer, shouldered his bag. He felt the buzz and told himself to be cool.

Taylor was sitting at the bar when Fox went out. He was in profile, a middy in front of him. Fox went to take a deep breath, told himself again to be cool, when Taylor turned his head as if he felt Fox's presence. His face had been blank, but that hint of a smile came over it when he saw Fox.

"Hey," he said.

"Hey," Fox tried to say back, but it sounded more like a grunt caught in phlegm.

Taylor frowned at him. "You're sick."

"I'm alright."

Taylor spun on his stool so he was facing him. He was big, but Fox's first impression had been right – he hunched in on himself. It made his long limbs and broad shoulders look less intimidating.

"Thought it was you," Taylor murmured like he'd been wondering about it since this morning.

"I'm good, you gonna finish that?" Fox said and leaned against the bar, head inclined at the beer.

Taylor kept watching him. "You want it?"

Fox didn't know why that made him flush, but it did, so he grabbed the beer and drank it in one go. He felt awkward. He was downing the dregs when he felt a drop catch in his throat the wrong way. He pulled the glass back and heaved a cough that started with his mouth pointed towards the ceiling and ended with him crouched and hacking, trying to suck in pulls of air.

Fox felt a hand go to his back, the broad palm rubbing his spine in smooth sweeps up and down.

The touch was firm as Taylor said, "Jesus, kid," right near his ear.

He heard Madison telling Taylor to "Give him a glass of water for fuck's sake," and Fox started to laugh in between the coughing.

Taylor's hand felt nice. It felt really nice.

Fox stood and knocked Taylor's hand off his back in the process. He wiped his mouth with his sleeve and turned. Taylor was standing now and he was close. Fox had to tilt his head back the tiniest bit to meet his eyes. Fox didn't have to do that very often.

"I'm good," he croaked.

Taylor frowned and lowered his voice, "I can do this on my own."

Fox shook his head. Taylor probably could, but it wasn't smart, and anyway, Fox needed the cash.

"I'm good."

At least he felt buzzed. He grabbed his backpack and was about to walk out when Taylor stopped him with the glass of water. Fox sipped it, clearing his throat a few times as the cool water slid down his throat. He handed the glass back. He didn't know why he did that – the bar was right there. Taylor took it, but he was still frowning. He was still beautiful.

Fox heard himself have that thought and told himself to shut the fuck up. He broke eye contact and made for the door.

"Yeah, bye to you too," Madison called out.

Fox lifted his hand in a wave and didn't look back. He felt the sting of how much of an asshole that made him and ignored it. He was still grunting and trying to clear his throat when he felt Taylor at his back.

"She likes you," Taylor said.

"Huh?"

"The girl at the bar."

That was such a crazy thing to say, it made Fox brave enough to look at him again. "Madison doesn't like poor boys."

"Is that what you are," Taylor said.

"This way," he said before Fox could reply.

Fox followed him to a black Valiant Charger. Restored.

Fox really wanted a cigarette.

"Ah, do you mind if?" Fox pulled his cigarettes out and lifted the packet.

Taylor glanced over his shoulder.

"You can smoke in the car," he said and unlocked it. The immobiliser beep-beeped into the empty carpark.

"Really?"

"Really."

Fox went around to the passenger door and opened it. He focused on getting in without looking like an absolute tool. It was nice inside. Clean and it smelled good, like pine and cleaner.

"You sure?" Fox said as he rolled the packet in his hands.

"I'm sure," Taylor replied and started the engine. It roared to life. That was a cliché, but that's what Fox thought as he heard the rumble then felt the purr.

"Dunno if you should with that cough though."

"Meh," Fox shrugged. "Whaddya gonna do?"

He hoped he sounded cool. Taylor gave him the side-eye. He seemed even bigger in the confined space. It's not like they were cramped in here – it was spacious and dark and Fox could stretch his long legs out and recline back – but he could feel Taylor beside him. His presence was warm, and his scent was clean with a hint of deodorant, like he'd showered just before he came to pick Fox up. Fox wondered where he lived, how far he had to drive. No one liked doing pick-ups or drop-offs in the hills. Fox had walked the escarpment many times. Once a guy in a ute even went so far as to take him to the bottom of the hill and then told him to get out and walk the rest of the way.

It's not like the hill was that steep or even that far. But maybe it was because everywhere else was so flat.

Fox lit his cigarette and inhaled around the tickle in his throat. He felt it catch, breathed awkwardly to stop it, and felt it pass. Taylor was focused on reversing, then swinging the car to face the roundabout, but Fox swore he could feel some of that attention on him. He blew the smoke out the crack in the window, cleared his throat and said nothing.

"Gotta pick up the gear," Taylor said as he cruised around the roundabout, the car taking it low and tight but it felt wide in that way big cars did.

Fox was surprised. Taylor answered his unspoken question.

"Territory."

Of course. Fox felt even stupider.

"Why'd you pick me up then?"

Taylor's eyes were on the road. He slowed as they approached the main road, indicator flicking left to take them back to the clubhouse. It'd be an hour roundtrip for Taylor.

"How else were you gonna get there?"

Fox was going to say, Kalum duh. Or the bus. Except no buses ran this late. Hell, he could've ridden his bike.

"I like going for a drive," Taylor said as Fox mumbled about riding his bike.

"Kid," Taylor said and glanced at him as he eased them around the final roundabout and cruised down the road towards the escarpment.

"Not a kid," Fox said to cover his embarrassment.

"You still a teenager?"

Fox said nothing. He'd turn twenty in a few days. He took a final drag on his cigarette and butted it out in the ashtray.

"Still a kid then."

Taylor wasn't smiling when he said it, but he said it like he was smiling on the inside.

Still, Fox wasn't going to let it stand. "It's not like you're old."

"Old enough."

Fox snorted. He looked at Taylor, his sharp profile under the orange streetlights, the slight curl to his dark hair that went down to his nape.

"Twenty-three," Taylor said and glanced at Fox with a smile. Fox didn't know what to do with that smile. No one fucking smiled in this group. No one.

"You're Tony's cousin?" Fox asked as they stopped at the T junction.

Taylor nodded. He wasn't smiling now. Fox didn't push it.

They pulled onto the main drag and Fox felt the car open up, picking up speed as it streamed down the hill.

"We got four drops, maybe five," Taylor said, glancing over his shoulder to check the blind spot as he went around a truck. "Junkies, mainly. If five works out, then it'll be interesting, but otherwise pretty standard."

"Weights?"

Taylor shot him a surprised look as he pulled back into the left lane. "Eight balls."

"Oh."

That was a lot of gear.

"They want weights they can buy it off the street," Taylor said. Now he sounded like Tony.

They drove in silence and Fox started to fidget with his hoodie strings.

"Tony got you selling weights?" Taylor asked just before they got there.

"Yeah," Fox replied.

Taylor frowned.

"At the laundromat?"

"Yeah. And the carpark at the servo. The pub, sometimes."

"Inside?"

Fox shook his head. "Carpark. Mostly."

Taylor didn't say anything else, but the silence was strained. Fox had known Taylor for less than a day, and what Austin and Tony and his mum thought of him aside, he wasn't totally fucking stupid. Taylor wouldn't be entrusted with five eight balls if he wasn't somewhat of a badass, probably a fucking asshole. But, as far as first impressions went, he also seemed nicer than most of these guys. Maybe not nicer, more like, he was paying attention and not totally threatened by what he saw everywhere. It made a pissed off Taylor all the more incongruous. And – and here Fox was fucking stupid – unexpected and therefore, disappointing.

Fox looked out the window as they pulled in. He unclipped his seatbelt, but Taylor stopped him with a, "Wait here."

And then he was gone. Fox sat back and watched him walk up the concrete driveway and open the door, the light and noise spilling out before he disappeared into the clubhouse as the door swung back. Fox lit another cigarette. He squeezed his eyes shut and willed the tiredness away. He was anxious enough the drowsiness wasn't going to overwhelm him. He smoked, managed the cough, and waited. He butted out the cigarette. And waited.

Fox felt a hand on his shoulder, a gentle shaking motion. "Fox."

Fox groaned and tried to shake the hand off.

A huff of air like a laugh came from beside him. "Fox, we're here."

Fox blinked his eyes open. Then he shot up and flailed his arms out, like he was preparing to hit someone. The hand released him.

Fox glared to his right. Taylor was sitting back, palms up, a deep frown on his face.

"You fell asleep," Taylor said.

"And you didn't wake me?" Fox sounded super pissed. He wasn't. He just woke up like that when he woke up in strange places.

"Figured you could use it," Taylor said, dismissive, but also like he wanted to know why Fox woke up swinging.

Fox nodded, ignored the unspoken question, hacked the wetness up from his chest and looked around. They were in the laundromat carpark. It was dark except for the sterile brightness of the laundry. There were no other cars.

Taylor stretched over the console and reached into the back seat. He came up with a bottle of water and handed it to Fox.

"Thanks."

Taylor nodded. A car pulled in. The headlights blinded Fox for a second before it swung and parked at the farthest spot from them. Fox capped the bottle and went to get out.

Taylor grabbed his arm. "They'll come over," he said. He looked like he wanted to say a lot more, but the car door was opening and a chick was getting out and straightening her skirt and making her way over. Fox reckoned she was young, but as she got closer he could see she might've been once but she was so worn down it was hard to tell. Rail thin, her eyes were tired but shrewd.

Taylor cracked his window.

"Tony's?" she said. Her voice was deep. Deeper than Fox expected.

Taylor nodded.

She stuck her hand down her skirt and pulled out a wad of bills and shoved them through the crack in the window.

"It's all there," she said.

Taylor nodded again and handed the notes to Fox. Fox took them, mindful not to scrunch his face up at where they'd been, and counted.

Taylor waited.

"We good?" he asked Fox.

The woman sighed. "I told you it's all there."

Taylor was watching her, but Fox felt like his attention was on him.

"We're good," Fox answered him.

Taylor nodded at Fox's feet, and Fox saw the strap for the bag under his seat. He leaned down, pulled out an eight ball and handed it to Taylor. Taylor passed it over and the woman snatched it and shoved it down her skirt.

"You going north?" Taylor asked.

"Yeah, all good, but," she said and walked off, got back in the car.

Taylor looked at Fox as whoever was driving her reversed and sped out of the carpark. Taylor's face was crinkled in a grossed out expression. Fox couldn't help it, he laughed.

"At least it's well-wrapped," Taylor said.

Fox laughed again and shook his head. "Fuck, man. How old do you reckon she was?"

"Probably thirty," Taylor said.

"Jesus."

"Yeah, well," Taylor said and leaned over Fox to tap the glovebox.

Fox felt a cold sweep over him when he saw the gun. A gun. An honest to god fucking gun.

"Put the cash in there," Taylor said and slid the empty car manual wallet out from under the gun.

The actual gun.

"You've got a gun," Fox said.

Taylor glanced at him, then back at the money wallet. "Nothing for you to worry about. Money goes in there."

Taylor sat back. Fox wasn't getting past the gun anytime soon, but he dutifully stashed the notes in the wallet, smoothing them out. He closed the glove compartment and sat back. Taylor was watching the street.

"Do you know how to use that?"

Taylor looked at him with that complete attention, but all he said was, "Yes."

Well, alright then. But.

"Fuck, man. If the cops catch us with that."

Taylor gave him an assessing look, like he was sizing him up. Fox tried not to feel like a little kid. Taylor turned, so his whole body was angled towards Fox.

Fox swallowed, tried to hide it. This was it, this was the moment when he met who he should've realised Taylor was from the start.

"Cops aren't gonna catch us with anything."

He was looking at Fox, his eyes shifting back and forth like they were searching Fox's. Fox swallowed again, for a different reason. Taylor blinked and looked away. He sat back and started the engine.

"Where are we going?"

"Home," Taylor said and rested his hand on Fox's headrest as he craned his neck back to reverse.

Home?

"You wanna go back to yours or crash at mine?" Taylor asked.

"What about the gear?"

Taylor sat back, the hand on the wheel shifting in a slow arc to right the tyres.

"Got it lined up for tomorrow."

Fox didn't know what to say to that. Weren't they supposed to shift this shit tonight?

"First drop-offs at Carousel carpark at nine," Taylor said and slowly made his way to the road, "so."

He was waiting for an answer. Fox did a quick mental calculation of the bus down the hill so he could get the train, or maybe Austin would give him a lift to the train station? If he did that, he'd be at Carousel by nine. Maybe. If he got his ass out of bed on time. But.

"You don't have to go back up the hill," Fox said.

"How bout I decide what I don't have to do," Taylor said. "Home it is."

He hit the indicator for left and cruised onto the road. Fox was a bit taken aback by the whole get it done tomorrow thing. Tony was going to lose his shit. He always made Kalum and Fox drop off by sunrise.

Fox looked out the windshield at Carousel in front of them, the neon shop signs bright above the empty carpark. It was one in the morning now. He might as well just sleep here. It'd probably be safer than turning up with the money at whatever time tomorrow.

The light changed and Taylor hit the accelerator, not speeding, just going, and Fox tried to form the sentence. He started fidgeting with his hoodie string again.

"Tony always makes us pay by five," he rushed out, loud and embarrassed in the silence of the car.

Taylor glanced at him, shrugged.

"If Tony wants it by five, he can fucken sell it all night himself."

Fox's mouth dropped open.

"He'll get his money tomorrow night after we take our cut," Taylor said and pulled smoothly onto the deserted street that cut between the suburbs and the industrial area.

"You told him that?"

"Well, he's gonna know when he gets it, won't he?" Taylor shot him a quick smile as he said it; it was a smile that said, fuck him and we're in this together, and Fox couldn't help grinning back.

Taylor's smile widened and then he refocused on the road. Shit, but this was dangerous stuff. But, if Taylor was doing it, well, what could Fox do?

"So, we're doing all the drops at Carousel then?" Fox asked. He was thinking that maybe he could sneak into Sanity and get a new game.

"No."

Taylor slowed for the red light and looked at Fox. "Maddington after that, then the McDonald's on Leach, then back to the food court in Thornlie, which. Sorry about that, I couldn't get that asshole to budge on the time, cos then we're back to Willagee if five pans out."

They were peeling onto the main drag that'd take them back to the hill and Fox said, "You're apologising to me?"

"Yeah, well. It's shit, going up and down like that."

Taylor squeezed the steering wheel and released his grip, his fingers lifting up and down on the wheel. Fox watched him out of the corner of his eye. They were at the base of the hill now, and Fox didn't know what to say. Maybe it was shit, back and forth across the suburban sprawl, but it was fucking shitter sitting at a laundromat all night. Or any of the other shitholes Tony sent them to.

"You got a shift tomorrow?"

"Huh? Oh, nah." Fox shook his head.

Taylor squeezed the wheel again, said, "Cool."

They were passing the servo and Fox directed Taylor to his house. The Valiant felt huge at the peak of their little hill before they descended down into the cul-de-sac.

"Nice spot," Taylor said.

"Rental."

Taylor nodded.

"Pick you up at eight."

Fox stopped grabbing for his bag. "You don't have to, I can get the train."

Taylor shrugged. "No big."

He was looking ahead at the dark street, the orange glow from the streetlights on the main road the only light before the darkness of the bush beyond it.

"Are you sure?" Fox felt compelled to check.

"Yeah, kid. Go get some sleep and take some fucking cough medicine or whatever shit people use for that," Taylor said as he turned to face Fox. He had the hint of a smile.

Fox shook his head and hid his answering smile under his hair. "Mum's a nurse, I'll be right," he said and opened the door.

"Good," Taylor said.

"Bye."

Fox got out. He thought Taylor said bye back, but he was slamming the door and making his way around the back of the car before he could be sure.

"**T**HERE'S A BLACK CAR out the front," Clarissa said.

"Fuck!"

Fox shovelled another mouthful of cereal into his mouth and dumped the bowl in the sink.

"Who is it?" Clarissa said at the same time as his mum said, "You shouldn't be drinking milk with that cough."

She was sitting at the little table, black coffee and cigarettes in front of her, still in her uniform. He knew what was coming next, so he grabbed his take-away coffee and tried to get out of there.

"Did you get paid yet?"

Fox stopped, and for some reason blurted out, "How come you never ask her to get a job?"

Clarissa gave him a hurt look that quickly morphed into fury. "Hey, fuck you!"

"Clarissa!" his mum said. But it worked – she shut the fuck up about it. He'd apologise to Clarissa later.

"Hey," Austin said as he strolled into the room and surveyed them all before heading for the coffee.

Fox nodded at him and then bolted for the door.

"What the fuck is his problem?" Clarissa was saying to the room and Fox could imagine Austin shrugging and his mum watching them and saying fuck all because she never got on their fucking cases about anything.

By the time he'd heaved himself up the practically vertical driveway, Taylor's car cranking up when Fox's head peeked over the top, he was fuming.

Fox went around the back to get to the passenger's side and open the door. It jammed a few times and he was yanking at it when he noticed Taylor's hand opening it from the inside.

The door swung open and just missed hitting him. Fox threw himself into the seat, threw his bag on the floor and then wrestled with the seatbelt.

"You alright?"

Fox glanced up. Taylor was still looming pretty close. Fox got caught up in the presence of him. God, he was big, and he smelled good, clean with that nice deodorant again. Fox felt even angrier.

"Yeah, man, I'm fucken fine. Just go."

Taylor raised his eyebrows at him, but sat back. Fuck. Fox probably needed to remember he was dealing with the sidekick of a drug dealing asshole in a gang that was pretty cool with beating the shit out of people.

"Sorry," Fox huffed once they were on their way.

Taylor glanced at him, frowning, then said, "Got you a coffee. But you've already got one, so."

"I'll have another one," Fox replied, rushed and awkward.

"Okay."

They drove in silence, Fox draining his own coffee and then starting in on the other one. It was white, no sugar. Fox screwed his face up but drank it anyway. He wriggled around in his seat, wound the window down a crack and lit a cigarette, hacked up some phlegm and tried to act normal.

"How're we gonna do this?" he finally said at the same time as Taylor said, "You live with your parents?"

"Oh, just Mum, my brother and sister," Fox replied as Taylor asked, "The drop?"

They exchanged a quick look and laughed. It was nice, Fox thought. He shook his head.

"You go."

"No, you were saying, your mum?"

"Yeah, just Mum, my older brother, Austin, and older sister, Clarissa."

"You get along?"

"Yeah, we're cool."

Taylor nodded.

Fox squirmed, but then asked even though he felt invasive and nervous, "You? Girlfriend?"

They were stopped at the lights. Fox could feel Taylor's eyes on him. Fox turned his head and met Taylor's gaze and tried to hold it. He wasn't sure if he'd been correct and Taylor's weird look was trying to tell him to mind his own fucking business, or if he was missing something. Fox swallowed.

Taylor watched him do it and then said, "No," before looking back to the road and accelerating in one motion.

"Just me," Taylor added after they'd been driving for a while.

"Oh, well, that's cool."

Thankfully, Taylor saved him from further embarrassing himself by answering his earlier question. The plan was both mundane and clandestine. The buyer – Taylor's word – would sit down next to them on the bench just outside the eastern entrance to Carousel.

"The boring end," Fox said.

"Is it?"

Fox nodded.

"Well, yeah. There."

This buyer would place their shopping bag down next to theirs and when he got up, he'd take theirs.

"No count check?"

"I know where this guy lives."

"Alrighty then," Fox said.

Taylor laughed. It was surprised and it made Fox grin over at him. Taylor smiled back as they slid into a parking spot.

They got out and Taylor went to the boot and opened it. Fox came up beside him. Five shopping bags and the cash wallet.

"Put that in your backpack," Taylor said and grabbed all the bags.

Fox grabbed the cash wallet and stashed it in his bag, zipping up.

He wondered if it'd look strange, them carrying shopping bags into the shopping centre – Myer bags, Sanity, "Supre, really?"

Taylor gave him a deadpan look. "Maybe you're shopping for your girlfriend."

"I don't have a girlfriend!"

Fox wasn't sure why he said it like that; he could totally have a girlfriend if he wanted, he had offers.

Taylor shrugged, slammed the boot. "Don't think this guy's gonna ask."

Taylor walked off slow enough that Fox could fall in beside him as they made their way to the entrance. There was an old lady sitting on one of the benches, but the opposite one was free. They sat. Taylor took the outside and Fox sat down as casually as he could. He did not pull off Taylor's sprawl. He put the bags at his left ankle and leaned back.

The old lady looked at them and scowled. Fox looked down. His heart was racing.

Taylor nudged him. "Relax," he said softly, then louder, "Did you get everything?"

"Yes?" Fox replied and then realised this conversation was for the old lady's benefit. "Oh, yes," he nodded.

Taylor rolled his eyes at him. Then he slouched down more and ran his arm along the back of the bench.

"I dunno man, I reckon your girl's gonna be pretty pissed about the G-string."

Fox blushed. He could feel it. He was going red.

"Bit presumptuous, don't you think?" Taylor squeezed his shoulder then, a lazy grin on his face.

Fox felt someone sit down on his left. Taylor's eyes flicked over Fox's shoulder, but he didn't move otherwise.

"At least you got the Korn," Taylor said, his gaze on Fox but his concentration on the person beside him.

And that comment made the current situation disappear. "What the fuck?" He caught himself just in time and made a fumbled correction, "I, you didn't get Korn."

Taylor focused on him, surprised. "You don't like them?"

"Fuck, no."

Jesus Christ, who did Taylor think he was.

Taylor was smiling. "Who do you like then?"

"Ministry, NIN, Deicide, Burzum, Cannibal Corpse," Fox shook his head in disgust. "Fucken Korn."

"We better go change it then." Taylor stood. "Grab the bags."

Fox turned to the bags. The same bags. Taylor was moving towards the entrance. Fox grabbed the bags and walked after him. The old lady was gone.

They walked through the shops.

"In the Sanity bag," Taylor said.

Fox's heart was still pounding, but it was excitement? Shit, but that was cool.

"We'll take the pub exit and double back."

Fox nodded. He liked that Taylor did that, told him what they were doing. Most of the guys expected you to just know. Then when you obviously didn't, they acted like you were fucking stupid.

"You wanna change that CD?" Taylor said as Fox made to turn left for the exit, Sanity on their right.

Fox glanced up at him, Taylor was smirking.

Fox gave a surprised laugh. "Later."

"You sure? You sounded pretty offended back there."

Fox thought about them, standing there in the bustle of shoppers, enough drugs to get them some serious prison time, and Taylor joking about his music taste like he genuinely gave a shit.

Fox didn't think there was really even a CD in there, Taylor was just enjoying himself. Who was this guy?

"It's cool."

"Alright, well, no bitching when I put it on in the car then," Taylor said and they went out.

When they got back to the car, Taylor rifled around in the Sanity bag, pulled out an envelope and slid it over to Fox, and then pulled out a CD.

Fox was taken aback. Taylor looked up at him and laughed.

When Fox met Taylor, yesterday, he did not think of him as a guy who laughed.

"Fucker!"

"Hey, I offered," Taylor said as he stood back and shut the boot.

Fox got in the car and when he'd imagined it, before, he'd imagined blowing out a terrified breath and trying not to gush about how fucking scary this was, doing all this shit in the day surrounded by people. Instead, he was trying to get past the shitshow pumping out of the speakers. Taylor laughed at him again.

He opened the console and handed Fox a CD wallet.

Fox opened it.

He started flicking through the sleeves and gasped. Gold. All of it.

He looked up, Taylor was focused on the road, but he seemed smug.

"Go for it."

"Fuck, yeah."

Fox stopped the noise and put on *Psalm 69*. He grinned at Taylor. Taylor grinned back and cranked up the volume. Fox lit a cigarette.

They cruised down to Maddington, Fox's knee bouncing in time to the beat. The second track came on and his head joined in; the sound filled the space in the car, cranking to the climax and he looked over at Taylor, who was smiling back at him and then they belted it out together.

Fox was close to headbanging when Taylor slowed and indicated right for the Maddington shopping centre, the traffic from the opposite direction a steady stream. Taylor tapped his fingers on the wheel in a rapid beat.

He brought the volume down slowly as he turned through a gap in the traffic.

"Fuck, love this album," Fox said.

"Yeah, Al Jorgensen," Taylor said and shook his head with a smile.

Fox hummed in agreement.

"Alright, this'll be much the same," Taylor told him as he parked. "Cept the guy's a bit of a fucken tweaker. Might be him or his woman, I dunno."

Fox nodded. "Better her?"

Taylor turned the ignition off. "Better him." He twisted his mouth in distaste as he said it.

It was her. Fox was sitting on the opposite bench from Taylor this time, shopping bags next to him. She was meant to take the Supre bag and fuck off, but Fox watched as this skank came up to Taylor, practically fell onto the bench next to him, arms going around his neck, and said, "Hey, baby."

Taylor startled. Fox saw Taylor see her coming, but maybe he wasn't expecting this much of a fuck up.

"Corinne, hey," Taylor said and gently pushed her back.

Fox looked away, like he didn't know them, but kept one eye on the action.

"You got my shit?" she said. Her voice was scratchy, high.

She was fucking high, Fox thought. A skeleton in a white dress.

Taylor smiled at her, but his, "What?" was feigned surprise with a hint of metal Fox hadn't heard before.

"Carn, baby, Jack sent me," she sat back as she said it, crossed her bony legs, and pulled out a cigarette. She looked like she was settling in for a cuppa and a chat in a living room, not doing a drug deal in the middle of the fucking day at a shopping centre.

She looked down to light her cigarette and Taylor flicked his gaze up to Fox. His face was blank, and it happened in a split second, but Fox saw his eyes flick to the carpark, back to Fox and then back to her as she looked up.

Fox grabbed the bags and walked away. His heart really was pounding this time. They hadn't made the deal. Were they gonna make the deal? He slowed his pace so he wouldn't be standing in a carpark with a bunch of bags like a loser, the morning sun beating down on him.

It was hot. Was it this hot earlier? He heard footsteps behind him and went to hurry when Taylor came up beside him.

"Quick," was all he said. It was all he needed to say. Fox hightailed it to the car.

Taylor unlocked it and Fox jumped in, bags at his feet. Taylor got in and slammed the door, jammed the key in the ignition, started it and pulled out, spinning the steering wheel before gliding out and back onto the road.

"Fucking junkies," Taylor said after a tense silence.

"What're we gonna do?"

Taylor glanced at him. "Whaddya mean? About them?"

"No, the gear."

Taylor shrugged. "Take it back."

Fox swallowed. He hated that he had this fear, but he did.

"Won't Tony be pissed?"

He kept his eyes out the window as he said it. Taylor didn't answer right away. Fox went to get a cigarette but that reminded him of that chick back there and he stopped.

They were turning onto the sideroad that'd take them to the highway south by the time Taylor spoke.

"Has Tony threatened you?"

Fox jerked. "No?"

Taylor did that thing where he flexed his fingers on the steering wheel. He looked angry.

"Look," Taylor finally said and paused. They were stopped at a red. He looked at Fox and continued, "Tony's my cousin and I love him, but I've known him my whole life and he's a fucking asshole, okay? If he's threatened you, I wanna know."

Fox shook his head. "Not like, not like you're saying."

Taylor frowned. "Just the usual shit then."

Taylor said it quietly, more to himself, and accelerated.

"Don't worry about the gear," Taylor said just before they pulled into the McDonald's. "Tony'll act all pissed, but he doesn't wanna sell to those idiots, okay?"

Fox shrugged, tried to look nonchalant about it. "Okay."

Taylor gave him another one of those glances. "I'm serious. And you don't have to deal with him, okay? I do that."

"Yeah, alright."

To Fox's surprise, Taylor manoeuvred into the drive-thru.

He didn't look at Fox as he said, "I hope you like McMuffins without meat."

Then he turned to the speaker and ordered two full breakfasts, no meat, two black coffees, one with four sugars, and ten hash browns.

Fox hoped the sugary nightmare wasn't meant for him, which was probably the most coherent of his thoughts, when Taylor said, "Hand me the plain brown bag. Fold it."

Fox rifled through the bags and did as he was told.

The girl at the register slid the window open, gave Taylor a smile and a wink, and handed over the coffees, then the food bags, and Taylor slid the brown bag alongside the food bag, fumbled it, mumbled, "Sorry," and then passed the food over to Fox and said, "Check it," just for him. The girl must've caught it though, because she rolled her eyes.

Fox opened the bag and saw the food plus an envelope. He opened it and flicked through the notes. Taylor was taking his change, then looking to Fox. Fox nodded.

"Thanks," he said to the girl.

"Thank you," she smiled and slammed the window closed.

"Ten hash browns, really?"

"How many people order ten hash browns?"

"And coffee with four sugars," Fox said and pulled out a hash brown. "You want one?"

"I'm good," Taylor replied. "Gonna eat at the next drop. You go ahead but."

Fox ate a hash brown and got the money out, slid it into the wallet in his bag.

He took out a muffin, and then something occurred to him.

"Hey, you like, don't have to answer this if you don't want."

Taylor gave him a look. "Go on."

Fox blushed, scoffed. "Nothing serious. I was just wondering when you organised all this. How? I mean, not like you have to tell me, but."

Fox took another bite. Chewed.

"You mean instead of sitting at the laundromat with a neon sign on my head telling the cops to come and bust me?"

Fox went redder and scowled.

"Hey, I'm not having a go at *you*," Taylor said.

"It's pretty fucking stupid, but."

"Yeah, well, so's not giving you the option to line up something else."

"Like you did?"

"Yeah."

Fox stuffed the wrappers in the bag and added it to the space at his feet.

"I spoke to em yesterday," Taylor said. "Told em the plan."

"And Tony was cool with that?"

Taylor scoffed. "Like I said, if he's not, he can fucken do this himself."

"You don't need the money?" Fox asked before he could stop himself.

"Oh, I need it," Taylor replied. "But I don't need it so bad I'm gonna go to prison over it. And neither should you."

Fox nodded. "Yeah, well, it's not like I plan to."

They crawled forward.

"We're gonna be late."

"Problem?"

"Not ours." Taylor smiled at him. He had a great smile. That was probably not a thought Fox should be having about another guy. He lit a cigarette and sipped a coffee to distract himself. He almost choked.

"Jesus fuck."

"Sweet?" Taylor was laughing, the fucker.

"It's sugar water."

"Yeah, and their coffee's the shittest."

They crawled through the highway bottleneck, then through the choked lanes, before Taylor cut through some suburban backroads to get them to Thornlie.

"This place has the best Pad Thai," Taylor said as they pulled in.

Jesus, they could be buddies going out for food, not doing a series of drug deals.

"Never had it," Fox said.

"No shit?"

Fox shook his head.

They parked and Taylor told him to keep the Myer bag on the outside of his leg. The place was pretty empty when they went in. It was a standard Asian food court – plain tables with bench seats, bare walls, an assortment of vendors just opening up, food steaming under glass.

"You want a Pad Thai?" Taylor asked as he herded Fox to a table.

"Yeah, alright," Fox replied and slid into the seat. "I got cash, hang on."

"Don't worry about it," Taylor said and went to the Thai counter.

Fox glanced around. There was an older guy at another table eating some kind of soup, and a couple at another one drinking some concoction and talking quietly.

Fox's eyes landed on Taylor's back, on his black shirt hanging loosely over his black jeans, the sleeves taut on his biceps. He was in great shape, Fox thought. He didn't think that was a bad thing to think about another guy, was it? He'd have to be blind not to notice that Taylor was hot. He saw the way the girls they'd been around so far looked at him. It just was. Taylor was physically blessed. Fox was tall. Now. He hadn't hit his growth spurt until he was seventeen, and now he was tallest of all the guys in his family except his dad. He wasn't skinny, but he wasn't built like Taylor either, even if they were almost the same height. Fox knew girls were into him, but he looked at Taylor and thought, girls were into him and Taylor would actually know what to do about it. Fox didn't. He felt awkward and clumsy. He needed a six-pack of beer to make out with someone. He looked at his hands on the table and frowned.

"It's good, I promise," Taylor said as he slid into the seat across from him.

Fox startled, rattled by his thoughts and Taylor in front of him. "What is?"

Taylor gestured behind him to the Thai booth. "The Pad Thai."

"Oh, yeah. My mum makes this egg noodle dish, it's good. She had some Vietnamese friend, an exception," Fox shrugged and willed himself to shut up.

Taylor just smiled, a small thing. "This'll be better."

"Your mum cook?"

Seriously, Fox would like to sew his mouth shut.

Taylor shuffled around, like he was getting comfortable. "My mum's dead."

"Sorry."

Taylor rested his hands on the table, clasped his fingers together and lifted his shoulders in a rolling motion. "'S alright. I grew up with Tony. Don't really remember her."

Fox managed to stop himself from voicing how that revelation hit him. He was beginning to feel comfortable with Taylor. But if Taylor grew up with Tony, then they had to be close.

Clarissa was an absolute bitch, and Austin was cool, but he could be a real asshole. Fox would still kill for them.

"You're a lot younger than Tony though," Fox said.

"Yeah," Taylor shook his head. "I thought he was one of his dad's friends when I was little."

Taylor rolled his shoulders again. "He was still an asshole back then."

Fox hid his smirk by looking down. He'd be a fool to trust Taylor. To believe this was anything more than bait. Kalum was dumb as shit, but even he'd be wary of this banter.

Their food came and Fox watched Taylor add all his condiments. Fox took a bite. He chewed, glanced up at Taylor watching him. He smiled and nodded. "'S good."

Taylor smiled, took a bite.

Fox felt cool air rush over his back as the door opened. Someone sat down at the table to his right. Taylor kept on eating, so Fox did too. Taylor asked him about his plans for later.

"You mean when we're done?"

"Yeah."

Fox chewed, swallowed. "Probably just play my game, hide from my mum."

"Hide. Why?"

Fox took a mouthful and debated how to answer. He didn't want to say – because she takes my pay cheque from my legitimate job every fortnight so I have to do this fucking shit to have any cash. It was fucking embarrassing.

"You know," he said instead of all that.

"You want a drink?"

Fox nodded, held up his hand and went for his wallet as Taylor got up.

"Nah, man, it's cool," Taylor said and winked. Fox blushed, looked down and hid his face in his hair.

He felt a rustle to his right and looked up into wide eyes, thick with eye-liner. The guy was a rail-thin, flaming queer and he was giving Fox a filthy smirk, a knowing in it. Fox blushed redder, and dropped his gaze; he coughed even though he didn't need to. He heard the guy cackle and the cool air rushed over his back again as the sound dimmed with him.

Taylor sat, sliding a bottle of water over to him.

"You see a doctor about that?"

Fox hacked another sound, shook his head. "Happens all the time. We're done here," he said and glanced at where the guy had been.

Taylor nodded, like he saw it all unfold. "We can eat. We got time."

Fox ate.

"You met Cisco then?"

When Fox looked up, Taylor was giving him a small smile, but there was something else in it, a defiance maybe.

"Uh, yeah."

Fox thought met was a stretch, but he'd seen the dude, yeah.

"Good guy," Taylor said.

"Yeah?"

Fox didn't know what the play here was.

"Yeah," Taylor said firmly.

Fox really felt like he was missing something.

"Cool," he went with and ate more.

He was looking down, but he felt like Taylor was waiting for more.

Fox pushed his plate away, cracked his water bottle, took a sip and said, "So, uh, you know him?"

Taylor mirrored his action with the plate and pulled out a cigarette, offered one to Fox. Fox took it.

"Yeah, went to school together. Cisco used to get beat up. I kicked the shit out of the kids who did it one time. He didn't get beat up anymore," Taylor lit his cigarette as he said it, then leaned forward to light Fox's.

Fox craned his head forward, cupped his palms around the light out of habit and his little fingers brushed against Taylor's thumb on the lighter. The flame crackled and he sat back and inhaled.

"That's pretty cool."

Taylor smiled at him, he was still sitting forward.

"It was."

Taylor sat back.

"Anyway, we been friends ever since."

"So how come you did this here?"

Taylor looked surprised by the question. "I don't want this shit at my place."

"Yeah, but. Go to his?"

Taylor frowned. "That's another good way to get caught. Look," he said and paused, took a drag, blew it out, "if you're gonna do this, and I don't reckon a good kid like you should, but if you are – "

Fox felt himself redden at the 'good' and the 'kid' part of that sentence. Taylor went on.

"Daylight. Busy places. Organise it beforehand and walk away if they can't be discreet like we did with that chick in Maddington."

"So you don't use then?"

Fox again surprised himself with the question. If Taylor was offended by the interrogation, he didn't show it.

"Fuck, no."

He sounded absolutely disgusted. He shook it off and tried to sound diplomatic with the follow-up.

"You?"

Fox shook his head. "Nah. Tried it. Didn't like it."

Taylor nodded. "Good."

"Anything?" Fox pushed. He didn't know what he wanted to hear. Well, yeah, he did. But he wouldn't even acknowledge it to himself.

"Booze. Pot sometimes," Taylor replied.

"So no Viagra then?"

It was out before he could stop it and Fox took a drag to cover it.

Taylor laughed. "Christ, no. I'm not that old."

Fox didn't mention that none of those guys were either and it didn't seem to be the point, did it?

Taylor sobered. "What you're really asking is do I take Viagra with the rest of them and bang strippers and whores all night like they do."

Fox butted out his cigarette and didn't look up.

"Is that something you're interested in?"

Taylor sounded genuinely curious. Fox scoffed. He knew he probably should be into that. Even Kalum banged on about wanting in on that.

"Nah," Fox said. He tried to sound dismissive and cool, but it came out croaked.

"Yeah, me neither."

He chanced a look up, Taylor was giving him a smile and a grossed out look all at once and Fox felt something ease up in himself and between them.

"Come on." Taylor stood, butting out his cigarette and pocketing the packet and his wallet. "Willagee awaits."

Fox laughed, even though it wasn't even funny, and followed Taylor out.

5

♥

T RUE TO HIS WORD, Fox was in his room gaming that night. Taylor dropped him home and said he'd bring back his cut after he'd dropped it all off. Fox hadn't pushed on going with him – the less he saw Tony the better – and he figured Taylor would get it to him next time he saw him.

Austin knocked on his door and said "Yo" at the same time as he pushed it open.

"Hey," Fox said as he kept playing.

"I made stir-fry if you want some," Austin said as he sat in the desk chair, bowl in hand.

"Cool, yeah."

Fox played and Austin ate, swivelling in the chair and occasionally giving instructions. Fox followed them, got up a few points, then died.

"Ah, fuck."

Austin laughed.

"Fox!" Clarissa shouted from the front of the house.

"Yeah?!"

He thought he heard her talking and then footsteps on the carpet coming closer.

"Some guy is here for you?" she said as she pushed the door all the way open.

Taylor was looming behind her. His eyes swept the room – Fox cross-legged on the floor, Austin behind him. He wasn't smiling. He just nodded and said, "Hey."

"Oh, uh, hey?"

Clarissa was leaning in the doorway, arms crossed over her chest and looking at Taylor with a polite expression; but Fox knew her – she was wary.

"This is my sister, Clarissa," Fox said.

"We met," Taylor replied, maybe smiling? Fox couldn't be sure, but then Austin said, "Hey," from behind him, introduced himself and got up.

"Hey," Taylor said back and Austin squeezed past Clarissa, her, "What?" met with a shake of Austin's head.

She followed Austin out and Taylor and Fox were left staring at each other. Fox was still sitting on the floor.

"What're you playing?"

"*Resident Evil 2*."

"Cool," Taylor said and then lower, "I got your cut. Can I come in?"

"Oh, yeah, course," Fox tossed the controller and got up. He and Taylor did an awkward shuffle as Fox went to go by him to shut the door and Taylor presumably went for the desk chair.

"Sorry," Fox said as he bumped Taylor's shoulder in the small space.

"'S cool." And that was definitely a smile as Taylor went to the side and let Fox pass but not without allowing the contact to happen.

Fox shut the door and turned as he heard the chair creak. Taylor was sitting, pulling the envelope out.

"You can count it," Taylor said as he stretched his arm out.

Fox took it. "I trust you."

"You shouldn't. Count it."

"I shouldn't trust you?"

"You shouldn't trust anyone. Well," Taylor rubbed his jaw and looked around the room, "maybe your family. They seem alright."

Fox huffed and sat on the bed. He scooted back until his back was against the wall and his legs were crossed. He tossed the money out and said, "Clarissa can be a real bitch, but she's good too, you know? And Austin can be a complete asshole, but he's cool."

"Mind if I smoke?"

"Go for it." Fox started counting. There was more than he expected.

"I think you overpaid me," Fox said, looking up.

Taylor took a drag. "Each one's six hundred after Tony cuts em, we're selling em for a thousand. Tony gets two hundred, we split the other two. Five hundred, that's your cut."

Fox narrowed his eyes. "Tony gives us fifty for each one. Each weight we sell for three hundred. Four weights in an eight ball. That's twelve hundred. We move eight, we get four hundred between me and Kalum."

Taylor butted out the cigarette and sat forward, shaking his head. "That fucken asshole. Two hundred."

"Okay, but we only sold four?"

"I took care of the other one."

"You met that chick again?"

Fox didn't like that and he wasn't sure if it was because she was an unpredictable junkie or a bunt slut all up in Taylor's business, but either way, he hated it.

Taylor gave him a distasteful look, his face twisting up comically.

Fox laughed. Taylor grinned.

"No, got another buyer."

"So, I owe you a hundred back then," Fox said and pulled out two fifty's.

"No," Taylor said, slow, "you came to that drop, not your fault it was a fucken bust."

"Yeah, but, you went and did more work."

Fox thrust the notes at him.

Taylor sat back. He laced his fingers over his stomach and gave Fox a long, thoughtful look. Fox waved the money at him, for lack of anything better to do.

"You earned that money," Taylor said. He drummed his fingers on his stomach.

"No, I didn't."

Fox was starting to feel the position he was sitting in, leaning forward like this.

"We go fifty-fifty." And before Fox could rebuke him further, he added, "Have you had dinner? I'm starving."

Fox sat back. "Austin made stir-fry."

"You want that or you wanna go out and eat," Taylor said as he stood. "We could get a beer?"

"Ah, yeah, alright." Fox was surprised. But he got his shit together, shouted down the hall that he was heading out, and Austin said, "Cool" from where he was sitting in the living room and eating more, and Clarissa screamed back from her room that he didn't need to "fucking shout!"

Fox recoiled and he saw Austin shaking his head; he peeked over at Taylor, who was quietly laughing.

They powered up the driveway and got into Taylor's car. The sound of Pink Floyd filled the space as Taylor revved the engine.

"Nice," Fox said.

"Yeah." Taylor gave him a smile and Fox smiled back and told himself to calm down. He did this sometimes, he reckoned, got a bit too excited when he made a new friend. It was just that he'd never made a friend as cool as Taylor before.

"Brick in the Wall" came on and Fox was telling the story about how his Year One teacher had them sing it in school uniform and march in place for the end of year assembly before he could stop and assess whether or not that was a cool story to tell.

"That's so fucking cool, man." Taylor grinned at him.

"Yeah, looking back," Fox replied and shook his head at the memory. "She was pretty cool."

Taylor pulled into the carpark behind the shops.

They got out and together made their way in unison to the alley between the shops that'd take them to the pub.

"You been up here much?" Fox asked.

"The hills?"

"Yeah."

"Pickering Brook," Taylor told him as they emerged on the street and went down the hill a bit. "Did some work there when I first came up to the city."

"On the orchards?"

Taylor held the door open for him. "Yep."

They snagged a dark table in the corner and Taylor told him he'd get the drinks.

"I'll get the next ones," Fox said.

"Yeah, alright." Taylor went to the bar.

Fox didn't need to look at the menu – he always got the same thing. He looked at Taylor instead. Which was probably pretty creepy considering it was the second time he'd done it today. Taylor had obviously changed since Fox saw him – slightly different black t-shirt, this one newer looking, and nicer jeans, also newer looking, tighter. Fox watched the girls at the bar checking him out, and saw some of the guys giving him a wary look. Some of the guys that included Kalum. Fox watched as Kalum studied Taylor with what he thought was his subtle look, saw Kalum recognise him, smile wide and go over to him at the bar. Typical Kalum – no shame, no hesitation.

Fox watched Taylor give him a sideways glance while he waited for their drinks, then turn more fully, say something, and then Kalum was turning and shouting, "Fox!"

Kalum walked over.

"Hey, man," Fox said.

"Fox!" Kalum yelled again.

So, he was drunk. Fox smiled up at him.

"Didn't know you were comin out tonight. I rang and Clarissa said you were out. Just that, 'he's out,' and she hung up on me." Kalum laughed like Fox's sister being a bitch to him was truly hilarious.

"You guys should come sit with us." Kalum waved his hand behind him.

Taylor came around Kalum with two middies, slid Fox's in front of him and then took his seat with his own.

"Maybe later, just gotta eat," Fox said.

"Cool, cool," Kalum replied.

Taylor sipped his beer, then sat back, eyes going from Fox to Kalum and then back to Fox.

"I'm just gonna," Kalum pointed over his shoulder, looked between them, grinned and then leaned forward and rubbed Fox's head, mussing up his hair, before wandering off with a laugh as Fox told him to fuck off.

"What a dick," Fox said as he sipped his beer.

Taylor smiled, drank his beer.

"You know what you want?" Taylor nodded at the board above the little window that took food orders.

"Chicken parma." Fox took another gulp of beer.

Taylor laughed, a real hearty one. "No kidding," he said as he settled down.

"What the fuck is wrong with a parma?"

Taylor held up his palms. "Nothing, man."

"Well, what cuisine are you having, Mr High-Class?" Fox asked, eyebrows raised.

Taylor craned his head back, his whole body leaning back in the chair. "Probably get the steak sandwich."

Fox laughed.

Taylor rocked back and stood. "One chicken parma," and he went to order.

Fox thought he'd either have to get the next two beers or be sure to pay Taylor back. He said as much when Taylor sat back down.

Taylor gave him an odd look. He shook his head and picked up his beer and the look was gone when he replied, "Don't worry about it."

"So, what do you get up to when you're not slinging drugs and working as a dish pig?" Taylor asked.

Now, from anyone else, that sentence would sound like a slight. But Taylor looked genuinely curious. He was sitting forward, lighting a cigarette and offering Fox one, his expression open and interested in the answer.

"Um, nothing. You know, gaming and shit," Fox said as he accepted the light.

"Yeah, but like," Taylor took a drag and ran a hand through his hair as he looked around the room, then back at Fox. "What do you want to do?"

Fox took a drag and thought about how he had no idea. About how he hated this fucking question. But Taylor hadn't asked it like his mum – full of accusation and the expectation that whatever it was, he'd fuck it up. He asked it like Fox was someone who could be doing something with his life. Should be.

He said the thing that he was too scared to talk about to anyone, but it just popped out, "Marine biology."

Taylor's eyebrows went up. "Yeah?"

"It's stupid," Fox shook his head and looked down, butted out the cigarette.

"Why?"

"Because like I could get in."

"Did you finish school?"

"Yeah, barely, marks were shit," Fox blew out a breath and leaned forward, took a gulp of beer and admitted, "Bridging course at Canning College. I applied."

Taylor didn't say anything, so Fox chanced a look up. It was scary – just lifting his head – but Taylor wasn't judging him, Fox didn't think. He was looking at him with a hint of curiosity, but otherwise that chill disengaged thing he had going on.

"I got in," Fox said, then smiled wryly.

"Yeah?"

"Wait til my mum finds out."

"She be happy then?" Taylor butted out his cigarette and leaned back as their food was placed on the table.

"Fox," Hayley said and smiled at him.

"Hey," Fox said. "You got close?"

"Yep," Hayley said and gave Taylor a quick glance and a polite smile before wandering off with an "Enjoy your meal" that sounded pretty fucking sarcastic.

Taylor cut his sandwich in half and continued, "So, your mum?"

"Yeah, she'll make fun of it." Fox took his knife and fork out of the serviette.

Taylor took a bite and chewed, frowning. He swallowed and asked, "Why?"

"Because she thinks I'm stupid."

Taylor looked surprised by that.

"But, you're not."

Fox was chewing and he slowed it down, eyes on Taylor, assessing. It was the first time he reckoned he felt confident enough to really size him up.

"You don't know me," Fox said after he swallowed.

Taylor scoffed. "No, but, I know stupid."

"So, anyway, marine biology." Taylor nodded like this was a perfectly normal goal for an almost twenty-year-old dish pig slash wannabe drug dealer. Dealer. Ha! He was practically a mule.

"How bout you?"

Taylor wiped his hands on his serviette and drained his beer.

"You're looking at it," he replied.

Fox frowned and looked down at his plate. He heard Taylor get up. Fox sat back and watched him move across the room, two fingers up at Hayley behind the bar. She acknowledged him and went to pour. Fox didn't miss her curious glance over to where he was sitting. He'd dated Hayley for all of a month, and she'd dumped his stupid ass when he made a lame comment about not wanting to push her for sex.

She'd been giving him curious looks ever since. He didn't know what to make of them and tried not to think about it.

Taylor came back and gave him his beer.

"It was my buy," Fox said. "I'll give you some money."

"Don't worry about it." Taylor sipped and then looked around the room.

Fox thought he was going to comment on the crowd. Fox knew half of them and recognised the other half. The assortment of public school kids who'd stuck around the hills after Year 12, a few of the private school kids. His year, Austin's, Clarissa's, younger than them now too. Fox waited for Taylor to say something about them. He didn't.

"I wanna run my own show," Taylor said, eyes drifting back to Fox.

Fox took a moment to pick up the thread.

"You mean dealing?"

Taylor shook his head. "Something on the land. Orchard. Farm. Fuck, winery if I'm feeling ambitious," he smiled as he finished. His eyes lit up as he spoke and the curve of his mouth was self-deprecating; and in that moment he looked so young, and handsome.

Fox felt himself blush, but the alcohol was good to him, and he managed a nod and a "That's so cool."

And he meant it, it was. He took a long drink and thought about it. Down south. Sprawling land and a pond maybe.

"You gonna get animals?"

"Well," Taylor looked thoughtful. "Orchards actually my preference. But yeah. A dog definitely."

"Definitely," Fox grinned.

"So when does Canning start?"

"Same as the school year?"

Taylor nodded. "Cool, thought maybe they'd do a summer thing."

Fox gave him a shocked look. Taylor laughed.

"I fucking hope not." Fox laughed too.

Taylor settled down, took another sip before he got up with, "Gotta piss."

Fox watched him walk away.

"Who's your friend?"

Hayley's voice startled him.

"Huh?"

Hayley rolled her eyes, but she was smiling, kind.

"Oh, just a guy from work."

"He works at the Kala?"

"Oh, no, side work."

She gave him a look that said, please tell me you're not still doing that and I'm not fucking stupid. Then it morphed into concern.

"Well, he seems alright, but be careful."

"Whaddya mean?"

"You know," she waved her hand.

Someone put Metallica on. It was loud. Fox leaned closer to hear what she said next. He didn't make it out, but he watched her look past him and heard the, "Later."

Fox turned back to where Taylor was sliding into the seat across from him.

"Interested?" Taylor asked. His voice sounded sharp.

"Huh?"

Fox had to lean forward to hear him. He didn't know why someone always ended up putting on this song. It was loud and overrated.

Taylor indicated the spot where Hayley had been. This close and Fox could smell him – cigarettes and that nice deodorant. He could really see his eyes too, they were an odd colour – not brown or green, but some combination.

"That chick was into you," Taylor said. It wasn't as sharp, but it wasn't exactly encouraging.

"Hayley?"

Taylor nodded.

Fox shook his head. "Nah, we went out for like a month? That's it. We're friends."

Taylor gave him another one of those looks Fox couldn't work out – surprised and pitying, kind of sad.

"Hey, you wanna get out of here?" Fox couldn't take much more of this noise. More Metallica.

Taylor nodded, finished his beer and then got up. Fox followed, but grabbed Taylor's wrist before he could make it out the door. Taylor twitched at the contact and then looked down to where Fox's fingers were wrapped around him. He looked up and Fox met his eyes. Fox didn't let go, just nodded at the bar and said, "Take-aways," and still didn't let go.

Taylor didn't shake him off. Fox squeezed and let go. He didn't know why he did that. His face was burning and he was clearing his throat with a cough as he turned back to the bar and got Hayley to bring him a six-pack. He could feel Taylor warm and close behind him.

The cold air outside hit him and Fox made some space between them as they headed for the car.

"You wanna go to the escarpment?" Fox asked.

Taylor lit a cigarette, breathed out. "Yeah."

Fox swallowed. He didn't know why he felt so nervous all of a sudden. They were just hanging out. And Taylor was cool. He'd seemed genuinely interested in Fox's lame ass uni plans. Fox felt safe with him. But not comfortable. Which made no sense.

"You okay?" Taylor asked as he unlocked the car.

"Yep, all good," Fox replied around the nerves in his throat.

They got in and Taylor didn't start the car. Fox waited. He fidgeted with the six-pack, peeling at the cardboard. Taylor blew out a breath and put the key in the ignition. The car started and Taylor didn't reverse.

"Are you okay?" Fox asked.

Taylor looked straight ahead, then he shot Fox another one of those weird looks, followed by a smile and said, "All good," parroting Fox.

The drive was dark and quiet and Fox felt an odd discomfort between them. He wanted it gone. He wanted them to be cool. Badly. He didn't know why. So, he talked. And talked and talked. About his stupid uni plan and how he wanted to work with scientists on like, science ships. And about how his mum always said he was stupid and lazy and how his dad scoffed when he heard she'd said that.

Taylor nodded along, smiled, frowned, laughed and by the time they parked, it was easy again.

"Fuck, hope there's no cops around," Taylor said as they got out.

"You got shit on you?"

"What?" Taylor looked at him as he sat on the hood and slid up until his back was resting on the windscreen. "Oh, no. I'm over."

"Just sleep here," Fox said as he mirrored Taylor's position and cracked them a beer each.

"You wanna bunk in the back seat?" Taylor asked and sipped, eyes on Fox.

Fox laughed; it felt forced because he didn't get why he liked the sound of that.

He looked out over the city, at the lights stretched out before them until it went dark where the ocean was. Fox drank his beer and lit a cigarette, offering Taylor one, and listened as Taylor talked about dropping out of school, working on the orchards, about how good it felt to have his own money, about how that feeling had never left him, the feeling of freedom.

By the time Taylor was dropping him home, Fox was thinking he'd never had a better night. Which was stupid – dinner at the pub and getting pissed at the escarpment was pretty standard. But, he hadn't.

"Thanks, man, that was awesome," he said, full of beer.

Taylor smiled at him. "Anytime," his voice was soft and Fox felt his skin flush and looked down.

"Fuck, I drank too much," he said to cover it.

Taylor huffed a laugh. "See you tomorrow."

"Tomorrow?" Fox looked up.

Taylor was making a face, displeased. "Tony's."

Fox grimaced. "Right. Fridays."

He fucking hated Fridays.

"Yeah," Taylor said. It sounded like he hated them too.

"You need a lift?" Taylor asked.

Fox shook his head. "I got a shift, Kalum always picks me up after."

Taylor nodded. "Alright, well, see you around midnight then."

"Yeah," Fox got out and paused.

He stuck his head back in. "Thanks. I really had a great time."

Taylor had one hand on the wheel, the other stretched along the console. His expression was the same chill one, but his eyes flicked back and forth on Fox's in that way they did before.

"Me too," he said.

Fox's heart pounded and he didn't know why. He pulled back and slammed the door. Taylor waited until he was down the driveway and opening the front door until Fox heard him drive off. He must've just waited, cos it's not like he could see from up there and Fox thought that was nice, like, just nice.

6

THE DOOR CLOSED BEHIND him, and Fox was smiling, a stupid grin on his face when his mum's voice reached him.

"Is that you?"

Her voice was scratchy and high-pitched, slurred. And she used his real name, which she knew he hated. His good mood fled out the door and back up the driveway and everything in him geared up for how to manage this unscathed.

"Yeah," he called and walked past the kitchen and saw her, sitting at the table with the phone, cigarettes and goon bag in front of her.

"Where've you been?"

She always looked weird like this – like she was trying to be the stern mother over the top of the absolutely shitfaced woman.

"Out."

"'Out', he says." She dragged on her cigarette. She always sucked the butt so tight the end was crushed under her lips and the tip flared, burned too quick.

"Yeah." He stuck his hands in his pockets, hunched his shoulders; he hated himself in that moment, for shrinking under her interrogation.

"I'm gonna go to bed."

"Hang on." She sat forward and crushed the cigarette. Her eyes weren't tracking, but she was still in there, Fox could feel it.

"Who have you been out with?"

"Just Kalum, you know."

She lit another cigarette and took a big drink.

"Do you think I'm stupid?"

"What? No?"

"Do you think I didn't hear that car? 'Kalum' he says." She took a drag, a drink. "Who were you out with and what were you doing?"

"Just the guys, just another guy, fuck, what's it matter?"

"Just another guy? What guy? What are you doing with a guy?"

She was sitting up now, eyes pinning him – or trying to – and fuck it all, he knew where this was going.

"Nothing, I'm going to bed."

"No, you're not. Get back here and tell me about these guys." And the way she said it, Christ, Fox felt it like an out of tune guitar strumming along his nerves.

He said nothing. But he didn't move.

"If your nanna was alive," she said into her wine glass, disgusted. She took a big drink and then she went for it. "If she was alive, do you know what she'd think of you? Do you?"

She was getting louder. Fox couldn't move. He felt Austin coming up the hall before he saw him.

"Fuck, give it up," Austin said as he came into the room. "Jesus Christ."

She swung her eyes to him, bleary. "And you. You think you're so fucking good. You're just the same lazy piece of shit as your father, just like your father."

"Yeah, yeah," Austin said, rolled his eyes and went to the sink.

She was on a rant now though, and Austin just stood there, a look of disdain and leering ridicule on his face as she went at him. Austin glanced over at Fox, quick, and Fox got moving. He got into his bedroom and slammed the door and locked it. His breaths were coming quick. Fuck, fuck, fuck. Why'd she always say that? Why'd she think that? He'd never done anything. He'd been looking at a guy too long at the movies – and yeah, the guy was hot, but everyone could see that, what did it matter that he was a guy noticing it? And he'd looked over and seen her watching him. She'd frowned. She never said anything, but it was like she'd seen everything or something in that moment. But there was nothing to see! Fox wanted to scream it at her. And now this shit whenever she was pissed.

She was still going. Fox heard Austin tell her to have another drink and his footsteps padded past Fox's door. A glass shattered on the wall outside his room and he flinched. He checked the lock, found it secure, and sat on his bed.

Fuck, and he'd told Taylor he wanted to study? He started laughing to himself and then he was cracking up. Taylor. Fuck, imagine if Taylor met his mum. Fox's hands started shaking at the thought of it. He could hear her yelling still, moving around. He looked at the clock. She'd pass out soon and Fox could get a glass of water. Have a piss.

He shifted further up the bed and pulled his Canning College application out of the top drawer of his bedside table, the handbook for UWA under it, and his stack of surfing magazines under that. Fox looked at the acceptance letter tucked inside the application and smoothed it out, set it aside. He flicked the course book open and ran his hand over the bookmarked page, read the units for the millionth time and sighed. He'd need to move out. He wished, also for the millionth time, that his dad lived in the city. But he didn't, and that was that. He shoved the papers and the handbook back in the drawer and flicked through the magazine. He looked at Kelly Slater in his wetsuit, unzipped and hanging at his hips; he was coming up the beach, eyes and smile somewhere off camera. He had a great body, Fox thought as he looked at him, sleek and tan. Taylor looked tan. Olive skin but with darker hair than Kelly. Longer, obviously; Kelly had a shaved head.

And this was all observation, wasn't it? Fox thought there was nothing wrong with that. He thought about Hayley, about her asking about Taylor. About going to dinner with Hayley. How it'd been fun, and he'd been nervous, at first. But not because he really liked her, but because he was out alone with someone, out doing what he was meant to do – like, date. He was nervous with Taylor too, but not because it was a date. Fox huffed a laugh at himself. He felt his dick stirring and rubbed himself idly. He wasn't thinking about anything in particular, just like he wanted to get off. He looked at Kelly and thought he'd like to look like that; that if he looked like that then he'd have no problems getting other people off – women – that he'd be into them and they'd be into him.

The house had gone quiet and he still needed to piss, but he undid his pants and slipped his hand inside and gripped himself. It was kind of uncomfortable, the two feelings, and he liked it. He thought about Hayley and then he thought that was wrong – she was his friend. He stroked himself and tried to think about tits. He looked at Kelly again and his hand moved faster. All that tan skin. He thought about Taylor, about Taylor really giving it to someone and he got harder, it hurt and it felt so good and he could see it – Taylor moving over some woman, pushing into her hard and deep and Fox came.

It took a while to catch his breath. He still needed to piss. He didn't think about anything else as he coughed. Then he sat up and went to the bathroom.

7

Fox handed Clarissa two hundred dollars as he left for his shift the next night.

"Give it to Mum," he said. "My pay."

She nodded. "Yeah, alright. Where are you going?"

He looked down at himself, at the standard issue pub shirt.

She rolled her eyes. "I meant after."

And Fox could never get a read on why she asked. If she wanted to go – he didn't think she did, she made it pretty clear how she felt about those guys – or if she wanted to tell him not to go – but that made less sense, they didn't do that.

"You know," he said, waved his hand.

She shook her head and got up, money in hand. "I'll give her the money, should get her off your ass for a while," and she went down the hall to her room.

Fox grabbed his shit – a change of clothes in his bag, a bottle of pre-mixed bourbon and coke to sip at work – and headed out. The bus was empty except for some guy in a suit near the front who gave Fox a glance and then looked down. Fox didn't know if that was a scared look, but Fox was more likely to get jumped than do the jumping. He still wasn't used to it – the fear from his height. He'd been a shrimp for so long.

Work passed in the blur of fun it always did when he was getting tipsy during it. Even the shit tunes pumping out of the pub buoyed him up. By the time he was throwing the towel over the sink, getting changed, and strolling out to meet Kalum, he was grinning.

"What're you smiling about?" Kalum grinned back at him.

"Nothin," Fox said and swung his bag over his shoulder.

"Yeah, yeah, you got something to smile about, you got Taylor."

Fox stuttered a step as they headed out the door.

"Huh?"

"I got fucken Tony all over my ass and you get Taylor. He seems cool," Kalum said as he unlocked the car.

"Oh yeah, Tony's fucked," Fox said as he got in.

"Fuck, man. He's worse than that."

Kalum started the car and headed down the hill, telling Fox all the ways Tony had been a fucking prick for the past two days.

"It's like," Kalum said as they paused at the lights, "he's worse the more you get to know him. People are usually better, aren't they?"

Fox didn't get to answer. He didn't think he was meant to. Kalum went on, "Like, don't tell Taylor any of this though, alright? I mean, I know you wouldn't, but Tony talks like Taylor's the best fucking guy and shit."

"Really?"

Fox wasn't sure, but he thought Taylor had kind of stuck it to Tony this week.

"Yeah, man. Like he's God's gift or something."

Fox didn't mention that the feeling wasn't mutual.

"Thank fuck it's just me and Carl now," Kalum said, grimacing.

Yeah, that wasn't much better, Fox didn't need to say, just like Kalum didn't need to explain that Tony had only involved himself to be a prick. Fox was glad he'd wound up with Taylor – he got the feeling Tony wouldn't try and pull that shit with Taylor even though he didn't really understand why he wouldn't beyond being related.

They parked a way down the street and made their way to the clubhouse. It was loud. It was always loud on Fridays.

Kalum pushed the door open and Fox immediately pretended he wasn't looking for Taylor. He scanned the room and then focused on the skimpies behind the bar. Candy was one of them. Top flicking up, practised smirk on her face as she pulled her bra back down and took the two dollars.

Fox followed Kalum to the bar and they wedged themselves in between an asshole and another asshole. Thankfully they were ignored. Candy came over with two beers, winked at Fox and walked off.

"How come she likes you?" Kalum was saying at the same time as Fox heard, "Hey," in that deep voice behind him.

Fox turned and Taylor was there, the not-smile on his face, and Fox said, "Hey," back and tried not to smile as well.

"Hey, man," Kalum said and extended his hand.

Fox panicked that Taylor would scoff at him like all these other assholes, but he didn't. He shook it and said, "Hey," and then asked Fox how his shift was.

"Good," Fox said.

"Good." Taylor brought his beer up and took a drink, his lips quirking as they wrapped around the rim.

Fox mirrored him, smiling as well.

"Riveting stuff," Kalum said, a grin on his face as he glanced around the room. "Fuck, I wish they'd invite more girls to these things. And not just the paid ones."

"You reckon the not paid ones wanna come to this?" Taylor asked and gestured around with his beer.

Fox laughed into his beer; fucking Taylor. It was like he saw what was and just said it.

"Better not say that to Tony," Fox said.

"I have, many times," Taylor replied and grinned at Fox for real then. Fox flushed and his stomach sparked.

Fox was trying to think of something to say before the cool moment between them fizzled out and he failed to fill it. Taylor's grin had settled into a warm smile, and Fox said the first thing that came into his brain.

"You got any pot?"

Taylor looked surprised.

"You wanna get stoned?"

Fox didn't. He didn't even like pot that much, outside of smoking up at home by himself with some beers and the TV.

"Who wants to get stoned?" Tony asked as he came out of fucking nowhere and clapped Taylor on the shoulder.

Taylor flinched, imperceptible if you weren't looking at him; and Tony was an asshole, but he wasn't stupid. He dropped his hand, but immediately turned the rejection onto Kalum and Fox. Fox could see it before it happened.

"We got some gear," Tony said. It was a challenge.

"I'm good," Fox said.

"I'm offering you free gear, kid. Why don't you come in the office, we'll get you sorted."

Fox resisted the urge to glance at Taylor. That's why he hated these things – everything felt like a fucking test.

"Nah, beers, you know," Fox said. He sounded lame. He couldn't quite hold Tony's glance as he gestured with his drink. God, did he have to look so pathetic in front of Taylor. Taylor, who was still saying nothing.

"Shit's uncut," Tony went on. Jesus, he was persistent tonight.

"Think he's good," Taylor said.

Fox chanced a look at Taylor. He was chill, like he was unaffected by everything. But Fox could feel his demeanour change around Tony. He just didn't get why Taylor was here. Doing this. He didn't fit.

"How bout you then?"

And Fox knew Taylor would shake that shit right off – but then he realised Tony was talking to Kalum. And he sounded fucking mean.

"Nah," Kalum shook his head, mumbled something.

"What's that?"

The air in the room was filling with tension and Fox couldn't stand it. He had it at home with his mum, he had it here with this shit. The only place he felt like he wasn't getting it lately was with Taylor.

"Another round?" Candy's voice came from behind him.

Fox glanced back. She was topless now. In another hour, she'd be naked.

"How bout you, beautiful? You wanna get on it?"

Fox saw something flash over her face, but then she flicked her hair, brushing off the feeling with the movement and smiled, coy. "Sure."

Candy turned back, said something to the other girl and came around the bar. All the guys looked at her as she walked over in her heels and lacy G-string. She came up beside Tony and he smiled at her. It was a terrifying look. Fox didn't watch them disappear into the office, but as the door shut, some of the tension leaked out of the room.

"Fuck," Kalum said low to Fox and made a face. Fox blew out a breath and returned the look.

"You really wanna get stoned?" Taylor asked.

He sounded completely unaffected by everything that'd just happened there.

Fox shrugged. "Not really here, no."

"What about not here?"

Fox finished his beer and picked up the fresh one. He was embarrassed by how weak he sounded when it came to getting stoned, but he decided to say it anyway.

"I don't like getting wasted when I'm out, you know? I dunno why I said that, before."

Kalum snickered. Fox elbowed him.

"Fox here likes to smoke up in bed on his own and jerk it."

Fox shoved him.

Kalum ignored it and said, wistful, "Man, I'd love to fuck when I was high."

Fox felt a wave of heat go through him and he had no idea why. He hid it by sculling his beer and peeking at Taylor as he brought the bottle down. Taylor was watching him; he looked like he was trying to repress a smile. He also looked as unsettled by Kalum's comment as Fox was.

"Well, I can't help you there," Taylor said.

Kalum laughed, big and loud, and Fox rolled his eyes to cover everything else he was feeling.

"But I got some pot if you wanna get out of here, go to mine," Taylor said.

"Fuck yeah, dude," Kalum replied.

"Fox?" Taylor asked.

"Um, yeah. Yeah. That'd be good."

"Fucking sweet, man," Kalum said and finished his beer and put it on the bar.

Taylor came forward and Fox felt the proximity and his heart fluttered. But then he realised Taylor was just putting his empty on the bar.

Taylor's arm brushed Fox's shoulder and Taylor mumbled, "Sorry."

"'S alright," Fox murmured into his neck.

Fox could feel his heart pounding and he felt like he was about to jump off a building.

Taylor pulled back and told Kalum to follow him as Kalum got his keys out.

They walked onto the street. It was dark and quiet and Taylor said, "I got beers, if you don't wanna."

Fox nodded. "Cool."

"Fuck that, I'm getting stoned. You got food?" Kalum asked.

Fox felt like he was waiting for Kalum to get punched at all times, and he didn't know Taylor well enough to know if he was like that, but all Taylor did was say, "Umm," like he was genuinely thinking about it, "I don't know."

"We can order pizza," Kalum said like it was decided. "Where do you live?"

"Hammie Hill," Taylor replied.

"Fuck, really?" Fox said as his brain calculated all the fucking driving Taylor had been doing to accommodate him.

"Yes?" Taylor said and glanced at Fox, like he was trying to sound confused. But Fox reckoned he knew what he meant and he was trying to hide it. Like he didn't want it pointed out.

"Nice, close to the beach," Kalum said.

"Yep." Taylor stopped at his car. "See you there."

He got in his car and Fox and Kalum walked down the road, Taylor's headlights backlighting them. Fox felt Taylor's eyes on him.

He glanced back, but he couldn't see anything. Kalum was talking about how Taylor was cool and thank fuck they didn't have to stay and fucking Tony, what a cunt, but Fox was barely listening; he was buzzing, his mind on Taylor watching him and his body alight with an energy he didn't understand and didn't want to think about.

8

TAYLOR SAT DOWN ON his couch so his knees were at Fox's eye level. They'd made it over to Taylor's without Fox's mood changing much from – holy shit, get it together! Get what together? He's a good guy, a friend, it's exciting to make a new friend. Taylor had let them into his tiny apartment on the second floor of a complex and said, "It's not much, but it's out of the way," and Fox got that he meant, it's out of the way of Tony and the rest of them. They didn't come down here. Kalum had gushed about how cool it was, and Fox had looked around and thought, it actually is. Mix-matched furniture like it'd all been salvaged or bought second-hand, posters of cool shit like NIN and Ministry album covers, some art Fox didn't get but liked, a rug in that Indian or Moroccan style, and a huge-ass stereo. Fox had taken a seat on the floor when Taylor told them to take a seat, leaving the couch open for Taylor, and Taylor had put the stereo on – Massive Attack, to which Fox raised his eyebrows and Taylor smiled at him and said it was good with the pot. And then he went into the kitchen, which Fox could see from the living area – and now Taylor was slipping in next to him, placing three beers and a pouch of tobacco on the coffee table.

"If you want," Taylor said.

"Fuck yeah," Kalum piped up and leaned forward for the pouch from his end of the table.

Taylor sat back and Fox felt his calf against his side, his knee and thigh at Fox's shoulder. Fox breathed in deep and reached for his beer.

Kalum started to roll a joint and apparently decided to abandon his fear and his filter. "Why's Tony such a fucking prick anyway?"

Taylor laughed, surprised, a deep sound that whooshed over Fox's shoulder. Fox shook his head.

Taylor took the joint when Kalum handed it to him and lit it as Kalum started on another one. Taylor looked thoughtful. He inhaled, held it, exhaled and said, "That's some good shit. Got it from an old lady down south."

"Yeah?" Kalum said, gaze focused on the joint he was rolling.

Taylor took another drag, another, then exhaled long and slow.

"Tony's dad was a mean motherfucker," Taylor said. It felt like it came out of nowhere. But of course he was just answering Kalum's question. Of course he was.

"But that's not it," Taylor went on. He ashed the joint and offered it to Fox, his full attention on him. "It's smooth. No paranoia shit. But only if you want."

"Yeah alright, one toke," Fox said and took it, his finger brushing Taylor's as he handed it over. Fox's eyes were on the joint, but he could feel Taylor's on him.

He took a drag, held it, and tried not to cough. He failed and coughed up a storm. He could hear Kalum laughing. He felt Taylor's hand on his back, kind of patting him and rubbing him at the same time.

Fox held the joint up and Taylor took it. Fox had a swig of beer.

"Fuck," he said when he could.

"You alright, man?" Kalum asked, unfazed.

"I'm good," Fox said and hacked up a few more times.

"You want some water?" Taylor asked. And Fox felt him moving to get it, and he felt it because Taylor's hand left his back.

"Nah, beer's good," Fox said and slumped against Taylor's thigh. Taylor stilled and Fox was about to sit up again when he felt Taylor relax and his hand come back; they were just reassuring taps on his shoulder, his fingers trailing along his nape, but Fox felt them lighting him up and he coughed and dropped his head between his knees. It gave Taylor access to move his hand higher and he did, softening the touch. Fox realised his action looked like an invitation and he didn't want to admit it was. Taylor's fingers brushed back and forth and Fox knew to the outside – to Kalum – it would look like nothing, a reassuring pat on the back, but it didn't feel like that. At all. Not to Fox. And he was pretty sure it didn't to Taylor either.

"If it's not cos of his dad," Kalum said, and he sounded thoughtful now too, which meant he was definitely wasted, "then what is it?"

Taylor's hand stopped moving, but he kept the contact – a small thing between Fox's shoulder blade and Taylor's hand.

"I reckon it was a run in he had when he was younger. Some bigger kids. Jumped him."

Taylor took another drag, held it, blew it out.

"Something like that, you let it go or you hold it in and it changes you."

Fox sat up and tipped his head back, Taylor looked down at him.

"He held it in," he finished.

Kalum hummed. "Still, doesn't mean he has an excuse to be such a prick."

Taylor's lips quirked. "Nah," he looked away from Fox to Kalum. "It doesn't."

"Let's order pizza," Kalum said.

"Menu's on the counter," Taylor said and didn't move. His hand was still resting near Fox's shoulder, and he brushed his forefinger back and forth. "Get me the veggie supreme."

Kalum got up and said he was getting the meat lovers and none of this shit about the Hawaiian, Fox, God.

"You don't like meat?" Fox asked.

"Don't like to eat pigs," Taylor replied.

"Why?"

Taylor smiled. Taylor wasn't 'cute' – he was a very manly dude, but his smile was cute when he said, "I like them."

"I've never met one," Fox said.

And yeah, he was stoned.

"You should, they're pretty cool."

Taylor was still smiling that smile when Kalum threw himself back down on the opposite couch.

"Well, I'm getting the meat lovers anyway, friendly pigs or not."

Fox laughed and Taylor grinned at him.

"Taylor you're getting the veggie supreme and Fox?"

"I'll share the veggie if that's cool?"

Taylor ran that finger along the skin above Fox's shirt. "Totally cool."

Fox shivered.

"Awesome." Kalum got up again.

"You good?" Taylor asked softly.

"Yeah?"

"I mean from the pot."

"Oh, yeah," Fox nodded and ducked his head, coughed a bit. "Yeah, it's good."

It was. Smooth. Not paranoia shit at all. Or maybe that was just Taylor's company.

"Good," Taylor said and sat back.

Kalum came back in and said it'd be half an hour and then asked Taylor where he was from and Fox listened as Taylor talked about down south and coming to the city to work when he was sixteen. His voice was nice. It was commanding and deep, but not overbearing, not trying to be anything other than what he was. Every now and then, Taylor would run his finger back and forth across Fox's skin. Fox wondered if Kalum noticed. He looked from Taylor to Kalum as he lit a cigarette and saw the way they were angled so that Kalum couldn't see anything. Kalum was sprawled back, lids drooping as he drank his beer anyway. Not that there was really anything to see – Fox had said pot could make him feel shit, and Taylor was being a good guy and making sure he was alright.

The pizza arrived and Kalum ate two slices and then passed out.

"He does that," Fox said and took another slice.

"He sure does," Taylor replied, and Fox met his eyes and laughed.

"He's a good guy," Fox said.

"He is."

Taylor took another slice too, his free hand slipping further down Fox's shoulder. Fox focused on chewing. With Kalum asleep – and Fox knew him, that was it, he was out – it felt like they were alone. And they were alone all the time, Fox reminded himself, nothing weird about it.

"This is really good," Fox said as he finished his slice.

"Place in Freo is better. We could go next time," Taylor said.

"Sounds good."

"Good." Taylor squeezed Fox's shoulder before removing his hand and reaching for his beer.

Fox felt the absence of the touch and sank back without thinking about what the fuck he was doing. The CD had rolled over to some ambient stuff. Taylor hadn't turned the main lights on when they arrived, just the lamp, and the room had a warm, cosy feel to it. Taylor asked if he wanted another beer and got up to get it. He handed it over and resettled against Fox's shoulder. He felt closer. He started talking about the album that was on. A Norwegian group. Asked if Fox liked it. Fox did. Said he'd have to tell Austin about it.

"Your brother?"

"Yeah."

"He seems alright."

"Yeah, he's cool."

Fox took a drink and said, "Mum stays out of his way so he runs interference for me a lot."

He didn't know why he said that. Taylor didn't want to hear about his shitty white trash family.

"She hassles you?"

Fox shrugged. "Yeah, but it's cool."

"Is it?"

Fox was gonna say, yeah, course, he wasn't gonna run his mum down. She was his mum. She was good to him as well. Wasn't all bad. He loved her. Course he did. He didn't know why he said what he said.

"No. She makes me feel like shit."

"How?"

Fox sucked in a breath. "Just like, you know. Like I'm shit."

"You're not," Taylor sounded quite vehement about it, in his quiet way.

"You don't know me, man," Fox replied and tipped his head down.

Taylor ran his hand over Fox's shoulder so his fingers were on Fox's collar bones, under his shirt.

"Not really, no."

Fox tried to keep his breathing even.

"But I," Taylor broke off. He ran his finger back and forth.

"You what?"

Taylor exhaled. It sounded really loud.

"I like you."

"I like you too," Fox rushed out. He glanced up and Taylor was watching him. He looked like he was waiting for something.

Taylor ran his fingers along Fox's collar bone, a light touch. Fox shivered and watched Taylor watch him do it. Fox didn't know what to say or do; he felt, shit, he felt turned on. Really turned on. So then he felt really fucking embarrassed. He looked away, looked down between his legs to where he could feel his dick stirring.

"You can crash here if you want," Taylor said and took his hand back.

Fox felt relieved and he wanted the touch back at the same time. He wanted to turn around and press up onto his knees and kiss Taylor. He wanted to push him back into the couch and climb into his lap and straddle him and kiss him, feel Taylor kissing him back. He coughed. He couldn't, he didn't, he'd never wanted that. He liked girls. Didn't he?

"Fox?"

"What?"

"You okay?"

"Yeah, good."

He coughed again. He reached for his beer and took a big drink.

"I gotta crash," Taylor said.

"Oh, okay."

Taylor didn't move though. Fox tried to get his dick and his heart and his body under control. He finished his beer.

"Hey, Fox?"

"Yeah?"

"You're alright, you know?"

Fox craned his head back to look over his shoulder. Taylor was sitting forward, his arms resting on his thighs, but he'd moved enough to give Fox some space.

Fox nodded. "Yeah, I'm good."

Taylor shook his head. "I mean, that shit with your mum? That's about her, you know that right?"

Fox frowned. He'd forgotten they'd even been talking about her. At least it would kill his boner.

But, he didn't believe that. Or think that. Taylor's hand came back, a firm press around his neck. Fox closed his eyes; he thought he was gonna cry, which was fucking mortifying. He felt Taylor's lips press against his hairline and he inhaled sharply.

"You're good," Taylor said as he pulled away, his breath warm against Fox's ear. Then he was getting up and moving away.

The music turned off. Taylor's feet padded around the room and then down the hall and Fox listened as his door closed.

Fox reckoned it might make him a coward, but he didn't open his eyes again until the apartment was completely still and quiet. He opened his eyes and told himself he was not going to jerk off in Taylor's bathroom about Taylor. In fact, he wasn't even going to think that fucking thought.

Taylor had thrown a blanket and a pillow on the couch behind him without Fox noticing, and he crawled under it and lay awake for a long time. His mind going over and over Taylor's hand on him, on Taylor's lips against his forehead, on Taylor in the bedroom down the hall. It was surreal. It couldn't mean what he thought it did.

What he was feeling? This wasn't what he felt. But he was feeling it. He thought about throwing this blanket off, going down the hall and getting into Taylor's bed, maybe waking him up, watching him roll over and say, "Fox?" soft and deep and confused and then when Fox kissed him, Taylor would press into it, his big hands would come up and pull Fox closer, pull Fox on top of him. Fox exhaled and it sounded really fucking loud in the quiet apartment. His dick was hard and he was cradling it, rubbing over the fabric.

Fuck. All of that turned him on. He fucking liked guys. One guy in particular.

Oh, fuck.

9

F OX HAD A PLAN for the morning. He was going to get up before Taylor, slap Kalum awake and get the fuck out of there. That plan was shot to shit when he woke to the sunlight beaming on his face, stumbled off the couch, and heard Taylor's deep, "Morning," from behind him.

Fox startled, spun around and said nothing.

"Coffee?" Taylor asked. He was standing in the kitchen, smiling.

"Piss," Fox replied and cringed.

He raced down the hallway and told himself to get it the fuck together. His heart was pounding. He went into the bathroom and slammed the door. He got his dick out. He was hard.

It's just morning wood! He screamed in his head as thoughts from the night before rushed over him. He tried to piss. Christ, he was like an old man in here. Taylor was probably wondering what he was doing.

He heard Kalum's voice. Then Taylor's deep rumble in reply. Kalum was saying something more, a lot of somethings. Fox inhaled deep, exhaled a long breath, and willed his dick down and finally got a stream happening. He heard Taylor laugh. He closed his eyes and shook himself. He tucked himself away, went to the mirror and looked at his reflection.

He looked like shit. His hair was sticking up, his eyes were bleary, and he looked pale, washed out. Fuck, as if Taylor would be into this. Not that he cared about that, because that was something he wasn't thinking about. He washed his face, tried to flatten his hair and then told his reflection to get it the fuck together. Taylor was his friend. He didn't want to get his ass kicked by an entire gang because he was hitting on a known associate. Cos Taylor was just being a good guy with all that touching. It's not like he was gay.

Not like Fox was gay either! He took a deep breath, told himself to get it together, and went out.

"You alright in there, princess?" Kalum said as he came out.

"Fuck off," Fox said.

"Some of us need to piss."

Fox had the sudden urge to tell him to hold it and get the fuck out of there.

But Kalum was wandering down the hall, talking about getting Maccas and the bathroom door was clicking shut and Fox was alone in the room with Taylor.

He turned slowly and said, "Hi," and then cringed at himself.

Taylor smiled at him, indulgent. "Hi. Coffee?"

"Um," Fox said. Christ almighty.

Fox watched as Taylor's smile grew, like he was enjoying this.

"Yes, coffee is, yes," Fox said.

Taylor laughed softly. "Coffee is good, yeah."

He slid the mug over and Fox took it, gulped a mouthful, choked and put the mug down.

"Hot," Fox said as Taylor asked, "What're you doing today?"

"I dunno," Fox replied at the same time as Kalum wandered back in saying, "Maccas!"

Fox watched as Taylor nodded like that made sense and then turned to rinse his mug. He wanted to ask what Taylor was doing. Ask him if he wanted to do something. He couldn't get the words out.

"You ready?" Kalum asked.

"Uh, yeah." Fox put his mug back down.

"Thanks for letting us crash, dude," Kalum said.

"'S cool," Taylor replied.

"Yeah, uh, thanks, for the blanket and shit, I didn't," Fox trailed off and shut his mouth.

"Anytime," Taylor said and walked towards the door.

Fox followed Kalum on autopilot. Taylor was opening the door and Kalum was giving him a back slap – leaning up to do it and Taylor gave him a grin and then turned his head to look at Fox. Fox walked up and paused as he heard Kalum belting down the stairs ahead of him.

"Thanks," he said again.

Fox wanted to turn his head. He could feel Taylor's warmth as he replied, "You're welcome."

Fox inhaled a shaky breath and felt stupidly weird. Probably more stupid.

"Later," Taylor said, voice soft.

And he was so close. Fox flicked his gaze up, and managed a, "Bye," as he met Taylor's small smile, his stance lazy in the doorway.

Fox made his feet move as Kalum shouted for him to "Hurry the fuck up!"

Fox tripped as he stepped out and Taylor's hand wrapped around his bicep, his body coming up close behind him. Fox had to force himself to keep moving around the embarrassment. Taylor squeezed and let him go and Fox managed to walk like a normal person.

Fox glanced back just before he took the first step and Taylor was there leaning in the doorway, watching him, a soft smile on his lips. Fox couldn't help it, he smiled back, shook his head and huffed a small laugh. Taylor's smile grew and Fox felt like something got exchanged between them. He turned and belted down the steps and felt light.

10

♥

AUSTIN WAS IN HIS room when Fox knocked, his soft, "'ello," coming through the wood as Fox pushed in. He was eating noodles.

"What're you doing?"

"Eating. Reading." Austin lifted up his book. *Dune.*

"Cool." Fox sighed as he threw himself into the desk chair.

"What's up?" Austin took a mouthful of noodles as he said it.

"Mum make that?"

Austin shook his head. "Mine."

"Cool."

"There's more on the stove."

"I'm good."

Fox leaned back in the chair and looked up at the ceiling. He and Kalum had been to Maccas, then they went to Hayley's cos Kalum said everyone was gonna be there for a swim. Fox swam. Then he shrugged off the calls of "Weak" and "Pussy" when he said he was heading out. He'd walked home.

The giddy feeling he'd had when he left Taylor's hadn't gone away.

"D'ya think," Fox said and stopped.

Austin didn't say anything. Fox heard the bowl clank on his bedside table as he set it aside.

"Do I think the old lady's a pain in the ass? Yeah," Austin said.

Fox laughed. "Yeah, but not that."

Fox blew out a breath and listened as Austin shuffled around.

Fox kept his eyes on the ceiling and rushed out, "D'ya think you know when you like someone?"

Austin rearranged himself some more and then said, "Whaddya mean? Do I know when I wanna fuck someone?"

Not exactly, but it was a start. "Yeah."

"Yeah, big titties," Austin said and Fox laughed.

"But you mean, like as in, wanna be with them," Austin said. He sounded awkward, which was fair enough, this was a conversation about actual feelings. They didn't do this, but they always could if they wanted. That was their relationship. This was always on the table, they just never took it.

But Fox was desperate. The buzzing under his skin, the pounding of his heart and the excitement in his throat; Christ, the swelling of his dick just thinking about Taylor – yeah, he needed some emoting.

"Yeah," Fox said.

"Yeah, I guess I wanna be round them all the time," Austin said as he moved around on the bed more. Fox could see him crossing his legs from the corner of his eye, his ankles sliding over each other.

Fox could check that box then.

But, "What if it's like that but it's a guy."

"Then you wanna suck his dick as well you mean?"

And Austin just like, said it. Fox felt himself shaking with nerves, but he managed a, "Yeah," cos he did. The thought of getting down on his knees for Taylor turned Fox on, made him feel tingly and so good, it was overwhelming.

"Taylor?" Austin asked.

Fox flinched, but he nodded.

"He's pretty hot."

Fox glanced at him. Austin was smirking.

"Get it, Fox."

Fox laughed and it turned hysterical fast. He calmed down before he cried and Austin said, "It's alright to be into dick, you know."

Fox nodded and he felt tears prick his eyes.

"Hey, have you guys," Clarissa said as she opened the door then stopped. "Are you crying?" she sounded horrified.

"No," Fox said.

"Fox wants to suck Taylor's dick," Austin offered.

Fox choked on air, but Clarissa hummed and said, "Nice. He's hot."

And Fox felt like he was having an out of body experience – was it really that cool?

Then Clarissa went on, "Be careful though."

Fox glanced at her – here it was.

"I just mean, is he alright-alright?" She leaned in the doorway. "Like, those guys he hangs with are fucking assholes."

"He's really nice," Fox said.

"Cool," Clarissa said. "Have you guys seen the hairdryer? I can't understand how it fucking moves, I left it in the bathroom."

"Why would we touch your hairdryer?" Austin asked.

"Yeah, I know, fuckhead. I'm just saying, it's gone."

"Mum probably pawned it," Austin said.

Clarissa looked like she'd been slapped. She rebooted fast and marched out again swearing and bitching.

"She definitely pawned it," Austin reiterated.

"Yeah." Fox felt a pang. He fucking hated this shit. And God, what if he dated Taylor and Taylor wanted to meet his family. His mum. If he saw this shit.

Wait. He was getting ahead of himself.

"Don't tell Mum," he said.

Austin scoffed. "As if I'd tell her you like cock."

Fox blushed. "Thanks."

"So, uh," Austin started after they'd been quiet for a minute.

Fox swung in the chair to face him. He still couldn't make eye contact, but he felt less like he wanted to run out of this conversation and more like, he could actually, maybe do this.

"You've banged girls," Austin said.

Fox nodded. "Yeah."

"So, you like both?"

Austin sounded like he was trying to have this conversation for Fox's sake, not like he was being invasive. He was sitting back, casual as always, but his voice was careful.

Fox scrunched up his face. "I like," he stopped, really thought about it. "When I was with Hayley, I liked her. And sex with girls was alright, I guess. But like, when I think about Taylor," he looked back up at the ceiling and blew out a breath.

"So, gay then. Cool," Austin said.

Fox nodded, even though he didn't know why or what he was nodding to. Or what to do next. He knew what he wanted to do. He sucked in a breath and asked the next question.

"D'ya reckon I should ask him out?"

"You mean like on a date?" Austin sounded surprised.

Fox tore his eyes from the ceiling. Austin was looking at Fox like he was missing something.

"Yeah," Fox replied.

"Aren't you already like, doing that?"

"Whaddya mean?"

Austin gestured out the door, as if to indicate Fox's room, the house, where Taylor had been. "He comes over, takes you out. Just the two of you."

"Yeah, but that's just friends. I don't even know if he's gay."

Austin looked thoughtful. "I dunno, I get the vibe he was like, taking you out."

Fox's mouth dropped open. He thought about all the meals, about the smiles, the touches.

"Shit," Fox said.

Austin smirked at him. "And you haven't even been putting out," he made a tsk sound and shook his head.

"Shut up," Fox felt his face flaming as he laughed.

"Well, she fucking pawned it," Clarissa said as she came back in.

"What're you laughing about?" she asked Fox.

"Nothing."

"Fox hasn't been putting out. How many dates?"

Fox could hear the grin in Austin's voice.

"Rude," Clarissa said.

"Shut up," Fox replied and got up.

He could hear Clarissa bitching about the hairdryer and then asking Austin for money and him telling her no fucking way if she was just gonna buy cigarettes with it and Fox went into his room, flopped face down on the bed and wondered what the fuck he was gonna do next.

Taylor had been low-key dating him. Maybe. It didn't feel real. Taylor. Hot as fuck and cool as shit wanted to go out with him. No way. Then he remembered he had Taylor's number.

He could call.

No, he couldn't call. What kind of loser would he be if he called? But then, they had no plans to see each other until Wednesday. Maybe Austin was wrong then. If they hadn't made any plans.

The phone rang. He heard Clarissa running up the hallway to get it. He'd call after Clarissa was finished talking to Daria. No doubt, it would be Daria. Which meant she'd be on the phone for hours. Fox sighed into his pillow and tried not to freak out.

"Fox!"

"What?" His heart thumped.

"Your boyfriend's on the phone!"

Fox scrambled off the bed and felt his heart pounding and his embarrassment rushing up and he crashed out of his room and hissed at her, "Shut the fuck up."

She smirked at him. "Kidding, it's Kalum."

Fox felt relieved and disappointed and took the receiver from her. She gave him a wink. She was still smirking.

"What," he said into the receiver.

"Fox?"

And that wasn't Kalum. He shot Clarissa a horrified look. Fox threw the ashtray at her and she cackled and ran down the hallway.

"Oh, Taylor, hey. Sorry, thought you were Kalum," Fox said.

"Oh," Taylor said and paused. Fox didn't know whether to explain or apologise, but Taylor beat him to it.

"So, Kalum's your boyfriend, then?"

"What? No! She just said that and then said it was Kalum and I said, what," Fox said and wished right now he said nothing else ever again.

Taylor didn't say anything. Fox could hear him breathing, and then Taylor said, "So, maybe she thought it was your boyfriend."

Fox swore he could hear a smile in his voice. Not a reprimand, not laughing it off, but a warm smile.

"Umm," Fox said. "Sorry, she's just, you know."

"Guessing?"

"Umm."

Taylor didn't say anything, but it wasn't a strained silence, Fox didn't think. It was a waiting each other out silence.

"Yeah, maybe," Fox finally said.

"Yeah, maybe it's your boyfriend?"

"Maybe."

"Maybe you want that?"

"I mean, it's a new thought," Fox said and wanted to kick himself. But Taylor laughed, low and amused.

"Is it?"

"I mean, yeah, in my head, you know? But not. Not like, everywhere else."

And with that sentence Fox really wanted to kick himself but Taylor hummed and said, "Yeah."

Fox realised then that he still had no clarity on what Taylor wanted.

"I mean, if that's. If you're interested in, um, that."

"I'm interested," Taylor said, no hesitation.

Fox blew out a breath. His heart was hammering. His dick was interested – just from this train wreck of a conversation – and he didn't know what do to with any of that.

"Hey, Fox?"

"Yeah?"

"Wanna go out with me?"

"Yes," Fox said, no hesitation, just his blush and zero chill.

"Cool." And that was definitely a smile in Taylor's voice.

They lapsed into listening to each other breathe again. Fox was smiling. He imagined Taylor was too.

"Pick you up tomorrow at nine if you're not busy?"

"At night?"

Fox felt disappointed. That was too long.

"I was thinking morning?"

"Oh, yeah, I'm not busy."

"Cool."

"Cool."

Then they both said nothing. Fox huffed a laugh and Taylor did the same.

"See you tomorrow then," Taylor finally said.

"Yeah. Yeah, sounds good," Fox managed.

"Bye, Fox."

"Bye, Taylor."

Thankfully, Taylor hung up first. Fox put the receiver down. He felt shaky in the best way, his heart hammering.

"I mean, if that's, if you're um," Clarissa mimicked from behind him.

Fox blushed and told her to fuck off. She laughed at him and dodged the notepad he threw at her.

11

F OX PULLED HIS SHIRT off and threw it on his bed in disgust.
Clarissa stopped in his doorway. She was still wearing last night's
clothes. Fox had heard her come in a few hours ago; he'd lain in bed
listening to her and Daria drinking and smoking and talking in the
living room.

"Wear the white shirt," she said.

Fox glanced at her, irritated. "I can't wear that one, it's fucking gay."

"You're fucking gay," she said and laughed.

"Shut up." He went for another black shirt on the bed.

She sighed. "Daria!"

"What?"

Daria wandered over and now he had two drunk bitches in his
doorway.

"Fox doesn't know what to wear on his date."

"That white shirt," Daria said coming in and going straight for his
wardrobe. "This one."

"Why that one?"

"You look buff in it," Daria said and held it up against him. He
towered over her. She was tiny anyway, but he really felt his size and
build next to her little Asian body.

Clarissa took a drag of her cigarette. "The black shirt makes you look, I dunno, small?"

Daria nodded. "Not small, but like, hunched in."

"Yeah, that. You want this guy to want you right?"

Fox shot her an incredulous look. Daria patted him on the arm. "She already told me. It's cool."

Fox went red, hung his head and cleared his throat. He'd barely slept and he wanted to tell them to get the fuck out of his room and he could say that to Clarissa, but Daria was too nice.

"Well, come on then," Clarissa said like she was waiting for him to put it on.

Daria joined her in the doorway, took the cigarette from her and had a drag before handing it back.

Fox huffed an annoyed sound, really hacked it up and out for their benefit, but he pulled his shirt off and pulled on the white one.

"Oh yeah," Daria said. "I'd fuck that."

"Eww," Clarissa said to her, then to Fox, "She's right, but."

There was a knock on the door.

"Fuck!" Fox said.

"Calm down," Clarissa told him and walked off.

Fox ran a hand through his hair and smoothed his shirt down and looked around for his boots and cigarettes and said, "Fuck, fuck, fuck."

"You look good, Fox. He'll wait," Daria said and Fox looked up. She gave him a warm smile; she was always so friendly and just, genuinely nice – Fox had no idea how she and Clarissa were even friends.

"Fox!" Clarissa bellowed as if she didn't know he was dramatically trying to get his shit together, like she hadn't been standing here annoying him five seconds ago.

"Coming!" he shouted.

He yanked on his boot, tied it, yanked on the other one, tied it, ran another hand through his hair, stood, shoved his cigarettes and wallet in his pockets, patted his pockets, and blew out an anxious breath.

He looked to the doorway, but Daria was gone. He could hear their voices in the entryway. He went out. He saw Taylor in the little foyer, standing tall and easy with his hands tucked loosely in his pockets; he was saying something about the beach.

Clarissa laughed, but Daria said, "No, that sounds really nice."

"What sounds nice?" Fox asked as he came up. He was nervous. God, he was so nervous.

"Nothing, your date," Clarissa said.

"Hey, Fox," Taylor said and Fox swore he looked shy when Clarissa said that.

"Hey," Fox replied. Taylor looked good, really good, and Fox's heart was thumping and he was trying to smile but he was nervous and overwhelmed by Taylor's presence.

"Alright, bye," Clarissa said and held the door open.

"You ready?" Taylor asked.

"Yeah, but beach?"

Fox wondered if he should change. But then Taylor was wearing those jeans again, a nice looking grey shirt, boots.

"You're good." Taylor smiled at him. He waited for Fox to walk out first, saying goodbye to Clarissa and Daria.

"Have fun," Clarissa said, sarcastic, and then slammed the door.

They powered up the driveway and Taylor said, "Your sister seems nice."

It broke the tension. Fox laughed and Taylor did too.

"She's a mean bitch, but she's alright," Fox said.

Taylor smiled at him, his head was tilted down at this angle – walking and slightly ahead – and his eyes crinkled and Fox wondered how he'd missed everything. How he'd missed that he was so into this, into Taylor. That Taylor was clearly, hopefully as much, into him.

"So, where are we going?" Fox asked as he went around the bonnet to get in the passenger's side.

"It's a surprise," Taylor said over the roof as he got in.

Fox didn't realise that was a thing – a date as a surprise. It made him feel giddy. In a good way.

"Yeah?" Fox said as he got in and did his seatbelt.

"Yeah," Taylor said and smiled at him as he turned the key in the ignition. His eyes flicked over Fox's shirt, and met his eyes again. "You look good."

Fox felt those nerves ramp back up but he was smiling too, looking down. "Thanks, um, you too. But you um, you always do, you know."

Taylor huffed a laugh and put the car in reverse. "Thanks. I never really think about it."

"You never think about how hot you are?"

Taylor laughed. "Well, no. But I'm glad you think so, I wasn't sure. You know."

Taylor was turning the wheel and taking the top of the hill in a wide arc, but he gestured with one of his big hands and Fox thought he got what he meant.

"Yeah, me neither."

Taylor asked about his day yesterday and Fox told him about Hayley's and walking home and talking to Austin. It looked like they were heading south, which didn't clue Fox into where they were going. It was Sunday, so traffic was light and Taylor hummed acknowledgements at Fox's boring narration. He thought he sounded boring. He was sure Taylor did something a lot more interesting. He asked.

"Not much, just worked out, went to the beach for a swim," he glanced at Fox, "worked up the nerve to call you."

"No way," Fox said. The giddy feeling was back.

"Way," Taylor replied and gave him another one of those quick smiles.

Taylor took an exit and Fox recognised Rockingham Road. He didn't have anything against Rockingham but like, there were nicer places. Not that he gave too much of a shit – he was with Taylor, he could probably take him to the refinery in Kwinana and Fox would be stoked.

"We're not going to Rockingham."

Fox looked around, felt bold. "I dunno, man. Kind of looks like we are."

"Just wait for it," Taylor said.

They wound deeper into the suburb until they were on the road along the beach. Taylor turned and drove until they were in front of a jetty, Penguin Island across the ocean in front of them.

"I booked the ferry and the penguin feeding, but we can probably walk over," Taylor was saying as he parked. He turned the car off, looked out at the ocean. "There's other stuff to see over there, thought we could see where the day takes us."

Fox was speechless. This was really fucking nice.

"I hope this is cool?" Taylor asked.

Fox looked at him. He was drumming his hands on the wheel, looking out. He looked young then. He *was* young, Fox remembered. Twenty-three was hardly old.

"This is fucking awesome," Fox said.

Taylor turned and smiled at him. "Yeah? Awesome."

Taylor shook his head and huffed a laugh, looked down; his hair fell over his face, and he sounded vulnerable in a way Fox couldn't have imagined when he mumbled, "Never really dated before."

And Fox didn't know why that lit him right up, but it did.

"Well, gold star for you, this is awesome."

Taylor smiled at him; he reached over and wrapped his hand around Fox's thigh, just above his knee. "Not quite gold star, but I know what I want now."

Fox gave him a confused look, he was distracted by the hand on his thigh.

"I've fucked girls," Taylor said.

Fox was lost.

"What?"

"Gold star? It means you're gay and never been with a woman. I have." Taylor squeezed again. "But not anymore."

"Really?"

"Really I've been with a woman, women, or really that's what it means?"

"The second one," Fox said. He didn't really want to hear about the women Taylor had been with. This was new, sure, but he already felt irritated by the thought of Taylor with some woman.

"Really."

Fox inhaled and decided to say what he wanted to say, "But definitely not anymore?"

Taylor squeezed again, leaned in close and said, "Definitely not anymore," right against the shell of Fox's ear.

"Come on," he said as he let go and opened his door. "Let's see some fucking penguins."

Taylor was right about walking over. They undid their boots sitting on the sand, tied the laces and swung them around their necks, rolled up their jeans and walked over on the sandbar. Taylor asked why he was into the ocean and Fox got carried away telling him about how he'd been into surfing when he was younger, how he was fascinated by the way the swells pounded Margs from every direction cos it jutted into the ocean, about how one time he was down there and a cyclone was happening up north and it just went crazy, which got him to thinking about what might've been happening underneath all of that, you know? What'd the fish do when that happened? Taylor listened. Fox wondered if he talked too much.

They got to the island and left their boots and pants as they were, and Taylor guided them to a little picnic table and told Fox to take a seat while he got out a thermos of coffee and two plastic mugs from his backpack.

Fox looked around, back at the mainland, at the blue of the ocean, at the seagulls flying up and cawing and dive bombing for fish, and he felt really fucking good.

Taylor slid Fox's coffee in front of him, shaking a packet of sugar into it and stirring with his finger. "White with one sugar," he said and Fox looked down at it, then up at Taylor, who was looking out at the view.

"Have you been like, dating me all this time?"

Fox wanted to shoot himself in the face after he said it. Austin might've said, but it was still pretty bloody presumptuous.

Taylor gave him a sheepish look though. "Kind of?"

Taylor picked up his coffee and took a sip; and that 'kind of' in that deep, uncertain voice made Fox's heart thump.

"Like," Taylor said and put the mug down. He met Fox's eyes and shrugged, smiled, and finished, "Yeah."

Fox smiled back, nodded. "Cool."

"Yeah?" Taylor's smile grew, still absurdly shy on his beautiful face.

"Yeah," Fox said and his voice cracked. He looked down.

"Cool," Taylor said and picked up his mug again.

They drank their coffees and went in for the next penguin feeding. Fox was not above getting excited over the penguins.

"Holy fucking shit, how small are they?" he said.

"Small," Taylor agreed.

Fox saw the girl feeding the penguins give them an odd look, but then he glanced around – Asian tourists and parents and kids – and he reckoned it was a couple of guys out of place, not a couple of gay guys on a date. Because that's what they were. Holy shit. Fox focused on the penguins instead of that.

Taylor asked the girl something as they went out and then told Fox to follow him and they headed for the other side of the island. There was no one around. The wind was cool and the air salty.

"Does anyone like, know?"

Taylor shook his head from where he was walking beside him. "I mean, not other than the guys I've, you know," he waved his hand.

"So you've like," Fox didn't want to say, "fucked other dudes." He didn't like the thought of it, which was ridiculous for a first – or third or whatever this was – date. But also because he was still struggling to get his head around it all. Himself. Taylor. If it didn't feel so right, so good, every other dubious thought in his brain would win.

"Fucked guys?"

Fox choked on a breath, but managed a nod.

"Yeah," Taylor said, he sounded a bit defensive.

"I haven't," Fox said as they came over the top of the dunes and below them, the seals. Sun baking. Rolling around.

"Wow," Fox said.

"Yeah."

They stood and watched in silence. Fox was super into the seals, they were cool as shit and usually stuck to Seal Island so it was incredible to see them here, but he also had this creeping inadequacy. He'd dropped that bit of information and maybe now Taylor would think he didn't want to deal with some kid who may or may not be able to go through with it.

"I'm not, you know," Fox said after a while.

He could feel Taylor watching him. Fox focused on a seal rolling back and forth on his back; not like he wanted to go anywhere, more like he was just enjoying himself.

"You're not?"

"A virgin," Fox said quickly.

He felt Taylor move closer to him, close enough that his finger brushed up the length of Fox's index finger and then down again.

"But you've never been with a guy," Taylor said, a statement, but the way he said it sucked the air from Fox's lungs and turned him on.

He shook his head.

"But you want to be," Taylor said and ran that finger up and down, up and down.

"Yeah," Fox said, it felt illicit. It felt fucking hot.

"With me," Taylor went on.

Fox nodded.

Taylor ran his hand around Fox's and tangled their fingers together, he squeezed and let go as he said, "Good."

Fox glanced at him, he felt exposed in that moment – shy and turned on and unsure – but Taylor was smiling, smug and playing it up and Fox laughed and shoved him.

"Fucker," he said as Taylor stumbled and laughed.

"Let's get through the rest of the date first," Taylor said and nudged Fox gently with his shoulder. "Make me work for it."

Fox wanted to say he was a sure thing at this point, but he didn't want to sound too slutty, so he just nudged Taylor back and walked close so their shoulders were brushing the whole way to the other side of the island to see the pelicans.

Taylor stayed closer after that. Not like, holding Fox's hand or anything – it might be the nineties, but this was still Perth, and it's not like it was totally cool for two guys, especially two guys like them, to be advertising that they were out on a date. But Taylor had leaned against Fox's back as they stood at the lookout and watched the pelicans in their nests, a warm line down Fox's spine as Fox whispered about how pelicans could fly two thousand kilometres, how he didn't get why everyone didn't crash their cars in awe when one flew over the freeway or slept on the lights on top of the causeway.

"'S pretty fucking cool," Taylor had murmured in his ear and Fox willed his breathing to a normal pace, then felt Taylor huff a laugh in his ear. Fox elbowed him. Taylor held onto his hip for a moment before suggesting they head back.

They caught the ferry, a careful space between them with Taylor's legs spread out, knees knocking like it was nothing, just mates hanging out for the day.

When they got in the car, Taylor exhaled and said, "I was thinking Freo for lunch," he trailed off.

Fox decided to be brave. Or no, his dick decided he couldn't wait that long, fuck his nerves.

"Or we could get dinner," he said and kept his eyes busy with his seatbelt.

He could feel Taylor's eyes on him.

"You sure?"

"Am I sure about dinner?" Fox asked with a bravado he wasn't feeling.

Taylor wrapped his hand around Fox's on the belt.

"I'm sure," Fox said before Taylor could change his mind.

"Fox," Taylor said.

Fox looked up and met his eyes. Taylor was close and his expression was kind, but it was also heated, and he was trying to hide it.

"Let's go to yours," Fox said, heart hammering.

Taylor flicked his eyes back and forth on Fox's. Fox made himself watch him back, breath short, heart pounding.

"Okay," Taylor said and sat back, started the car.

The drive back was a new kind of torture. Fox had never felt this wound up over the prospect of sex. Taylor put on a CD – Fear Factory – and Fox wanted to comment, to say he saw them at the Big Day Out, but he couldn't get his mouth to work. There was a tension and Fox knew Taylor was feeling it too.

Taylor parked and Fox got out and stood and met Taylor's eyes over the top of the car. They stayed like that for a moment, staring at each other in the early afternoon sun, until Taylor quirked his lips and said, "I've got beer."

"Fuck, good," Fox said in a rush and Taylor laughed.

He followed Taylor up the stairs and caught himself looking at Taylor's ass and then tried not to and then thought that was a thing he could do now, wasn't it? He needed that beer.

Taylor unlocked the door, stepped back to let Fox in; Taylor was careful not to touch him and Fox went in, heard the door close behind him, and went around to the other side of the kitchen bench. Taylor's keys clanged in the bowl and he went to the fridge. He pulled out two beers and cracked one and handed it to Fox.

"Thanks," Fox said and took a drink.

He lowered the bottle and saw Taylor drinking. Fox watched him as he brought it down and leaned against the other side of the bench.

"Tunes," Taylor said and went for the stereo. Fox trailed behind him and took a seat on the couch.

NIN's *The Downward Spiral* cranked on, low, and Fox tried to relax. Then he thought of the fifth track and laughed.

"What?" Taylor asked as he came around the couch and took a seat next to Fox.

"I wanna fuck you like an animal?"

Taylor raised an eyebrow and laughed, surprised. "I didn't even think that."

"Subconscious." Fox took another drink.

"It's actually about self-hatred," Taylor said.

"Closer?"

"Yeah."

Fox sat back and Taylor stayed forward, body angled slightly so he was sitting above Fox, but not too close.

"Depressing," Fox said.

Taylor huffed a laugh; his hair was hanging over his face and his eyes crinkled as he looked back and down at Fox. "We'll pretend it's just about fucking."

Taylor said it like a joke, but Fox felt those nerves again and something else. Something like he really wanted more. A touch. To touch. He put his beer in his left hand and reached out with his right until his hand was draped over Taylor's thigh, fingers dragging along the fabric. He watched Taylor look down at the touch, and then up through the fall of his dark hair over his shoulder.

Fox watched him and felt his lips part. Taylor flicked his eyes down to Fox's lips then back up to his eyes. Taylor placed his beer on the coffee table and angled his body so he was closer, his eyes never leaving Fox's. Fox's breathing sounded loud in his ears and he watched as Taylor leaned in. Fox pushed up to meet him; not thinking, just doing, feeling. His lips touched Taylor's in a brush and then moved back. Fox pressed in again and Taylor met him. Taylor's lips were soft against his and his breath was hot and it mingled with Fox's as they did it again. As they moved back, Fox opened his eyes and met Taylor's for a second and something passed between them, and then he was sliding his eyes closed and meeting Taylor for more. Taylor's hand came up to the nape of his neck and slid up. His fingers were warm and solid and when he deepened the kiss, held his lips against Fox's, Fox parted his lips and met Taylor's flick of tongue. He moaned and Taylor responded, pushing Fox back into the cushions with a groan and going for it.

Fox fell back into the couch as Taylor moved over the top of him, his body a hot and heavy weight pressing him into the cushions. Their kisses deepened, bodies moving in a rocking motion. Fox slid his hands up Taylor's back and pulled him closer. Taylor went with it, his hand still behind Fox's head while his other arm was holding his lower back and pulling him in. It was the best kissing Fox had ever had and he never wanted it to stop. Just this – mouths moving together, lips touching and tongues entangling – it set up a heat in his groin that radiated up his chest, made his heart pump and his throat ache. Taylor ground down and Fox felt his hard dick grind against his own and he gasped.

Taylor pulled back and met his eyes. "Bedroom?"

"Fuck, yes."

Taylor didn't waste any time – he pushed himself up, grabbed Fox's hand and yanked him up until he was chest to chest with him. Taylor kissed him hard and fast and then tugged him down the hall to his room. Fox tried not to trip over his own feet. Taylor was squeezing and releasing his hold on his hand. He pushed his door open and turned to meet Fox for another heated kiss as they stumbled into the room.

Fox moaned and slid his hands under Taylor's shirt, felt all that unblemished skin, smooth and hard and so much of it. Not like a woman at all. The thought made him groan and kiss harder.

"What do you want?" Taylor broke away to ask.

"Everything," Fox said and kissed Taylor again.

Taylor pushed his hands under Fox's shirt until it was under his armpits and Fox had to pull back to let him tug it off. As soon as his head and arms were free, he went for Taylor's shirt and pulled it over his head. Fox ran his hands over Taylor's chest – so firm and tan – he leaned in to kiss his nipple and Taylor groaned and wrapped his hands around Fox's skull.

Fox went for Taylor's pants and unbuckled his belt, undid the buttons and then glanced up and met Taylor's eyes and kissed him as he snaked his hand inside and wrapped it around Taylor's dick. It was hard and big and it felt fucking amazing in his palm. Fox whined into their kiss and he had a split second to feel embarrassed for himself, but then Taylor groaned deep and desperate into Fox's mouth and got his hand on Fox's dick over his pants and squeezed and Fox gasped, breaking the kiss.

Taylor shuffled them forward until he was toppling them onto the bed. They landed on their sides, bodies pressed close, and Taylor got Fox's pants open and helped him shimmy them down his hips while Fox did the same to Taylor's. They pressed back at the same time and Fox felt his cock rub up against Taylor's and he moaned, desperate for it. Taylor kissed him deep and angled them so he was slightly on top and then licked his palm, brought it down and wrapped his hand around both of them. Fox thrust into the slickness of Taylor's hand, the incredible glide of his dick against Taylor's; he kissed him and ground into his hand, into his dick. He felt his balls draw up tight, felt his orgasm rushing up too fast and he broke the kiss to pant, "Fuck."

Taylor increased the pace and force of his hips, grinding them together. Fox met him with a brutal thrust and came. Taylor kissed him through it and then broke away. Fox cracked his eyes open and watched as Taylor panted, squeezed his eyes closed and came with a small gasp.

Taylor opened his eyes, his lips parted. Fox kissed him. Taylor kissed him back and it was really fucking nice. Just coming down, kissing, stroking. Then Fox pulled back to laugh.

"What?" Taylor asked, he was smiling down at him.

"We didn't even get our boots off," Fox said.

Taylor glanced down the bed then back up at Fox with a grin. "Good?"

"Fuck yeah," Fox said.

Taylor ran his hand down Fox's chest. Fox shivered. Taylor gave him a sly smile.

"Let's get our shoes off this time," Taylor said. He leaned down the bed and undid Fox's laces. Fox brought his hand up and ran it down Taylor's spine. Taylor glanced over his shoulder and smiled as he tugged the boot off. The afternoon light was streaming through the white curtains, Taylor's head lit up with it. His smile made Fox's heart clench. Fox smiled back and Taylor returned to getting the boot off.

Once they were barefoot, Taylor took his pants off, pulled Fox's down and off and leaned down for his shirt. He wiped Fox down, then himself before climbing up the bed so he was over Fox. Fox moved back and lay flat with the movement. Taylor braced himself and smiled down at him. His loose curls hung around his face and he still had that smile.

"Hi," Fox said.

"Hi," Taylor replied, smile widening.

Fox waited. Taylor watched. Fox brought his hands up and ran them down Taylor's sides; he watched as Taylor trembled, his eyes never leaving Fox's. Fox brought his hands to his ass. Fuck, it was a great ass – he let his fingers trail in a light motion until he moved one down to tease near Taylor's entrance.

Taylor shuddered. "I've never."

Fox breathed out slowly as he let his finger drift lower.

"Never been fucked?"

Taylor shook his head and pressed back against Fox's finger.

"You do the fucking?" Fox felt daring, but also kind of pissed off, like he was jealous.

"Yeah," Taylor breathed. His body was moving in tiny increments into Fox's hand, his arms trembling from holding the position.

Fox drifted his hands around to Taylor's hips to his groin and slid them past Taylor's cock in a tease and then up his chest. He leaned up and took a kiss. Taylor met him, his body blanketing Fox's as he let his weight pin him to the bed. Fox adjusted his legs so Taylor was cradled between his thighs. He thought the position would make him feel like a girl, weak. It didn't. It just felt amazing. Making out, naked skin against naked skin. He wanted to stay here and do this all night.

He pulled back. "Hey."

Taylor rolled so he was still on top of Fox, but more to the side, his leg swung over Fox's, tangling them together. He pushed the hair off Fox's face. Fox could feel Taylor's dick – hardening and sliding against Fox's thigh almost like Taylor wasn't aware he was doing it. Fox had to reach down and give himself a stroke.

"Let's order in."

"Yeah?"

"Yeah," Fox breathed. Fuck, he was so ready to go again.

"But I had plans," Taylor said and wrapped his hand around Fox's on his dick.

Fox arched into it. "Fuck that, I'm a sure thing."

"Yeah, you are," Taylor said and smirked. The rocking motion of his hips undermined the sass a bit.

"Please," Fox said.

Taylor lost the smirk. He let go of Fox's dick and brought his hand up to his jaw. He trailed his thumb on Fox's bottom lip and Fox panted, let his tongue dart out.

"You ever suck dick before?"

Fox blushed. "You know I haven't."

"Want me to show you?"

Fox gripped his dick. "Yes."

Taylor gave him a hard kiss and then trailed his way down Fox's chest with teasing kisses. He knocked Fox's hand away and replaced it with his tongue. Fox groaned. Taylor licked up and down his shaft before wrapping his lips around the head and sinking all the way down. Fox arched up and Taylor brought an arm up and held his hips down. Hard. Fox gasped. The strength was so fucking hot and then Taylor's mouth, taking him apart, sucking him so good, he couldn't –

"Fuck, I'm gonna," he gasped and tried to arch up, but he was pinned and he was coming and Taylor was swallowing him down, his hips rutting against the bed between Fox's legs.

Fox was breathless when Taylor shimmied back up to him. Taylor's dick trailed over his abdomen as he came up and kissed Fox desperately.

Fox wanted so bad to make Taylor feel good in that moment – he pushed at Taylor's chest until Taylor startled and pulled back. Fox shoved him so their positions were reversed and he went down the bed.

"Sorry if it's bad," Fox said before he told himself not to overthink it and went for it. He drew the tip into his mouth and Taylor groaned. Fox sucked lightly and then tried to push down. He choked.

Taylor's hand came into his hair and tugged. "Use your hand," he said.

Fox got the message. He brought his fingers around the base and stroked at the same time as he worked the head. Taylor's hand stayed in his hair. Not pushing, just gripping; releasing as he groaned, then gripping again as he gasped. He kept his hips still. Fox increased his suction and then pulled off and Taylor moaned. Fox came back in and sucked gently, then got a rhythm going. He felt it before Taylor said it – his balls drawing up tight, his abs clenching, his voice strained, "I'm gonna."

Fox sucked harder and felt the come hit his tongue. He licked harder, drank it; he felt filthy, lost in the moment. He sucked Taylor clean until Taylor grabbed him by the arm and yanked him up the bed and kissed him.

"So good," Fox said as he broke the kiss.

"Yeah?" Taylor said, a genuine question.

"Yeah," Fox said and grinned.

Taylor held him tight and said, "We're ordering in."

12

F OX DIDN'T WANT TO go home – constantly fucking someone
he really, really wanted made it so much better, he wanted to stay
and keep doing it. But, he had a shift on Tuesday night and he worried
that Taylor would get sick of him.

"See you Wednesday?" Taylor asked as he put the car in park at the
top of Fox's driveway.

"Yeah," Fox replied. He didn't unclip his seatbelt.

Taylor blew out a breath and said, "I wish."

Fox looked over at him. "You wish what?"

Taylor gave him a self-deprecating smile and said, "It's stupid, but
I wish we could, you know. Just stay."

So, maybe not so sick of him. Fox smiled, shy. "Yeah?"

"Yeah."

"Can I stay over Wednesday?" Fox asked.

"Course. Yeah, that'd be," Taylor shook his head. "That'd be awesome," he finished around another self-deprecating smile.

"I'll take you out for breakfast," Fox said. He felt fluttery and bold
with it.

"Cool." Taylor glanced out the windows, quick. He leaned over the
console and gave Fox a hard kiss.

Fox pressed into it, and then Taylor was pulling back and he wanted to chase him, but they were at his house, in public, and he didn't know if they were ever going to do this in public. They hadn't talked about it. They hadn't talked about anything, much really, Fox realised as he got out and said, "Bye," and shut the door on Taylor's, "Later, Fox."

Fox headed down the driveway, turned back and gave an embarrassing little wave before shaking his head at himself and walking until he was out of view. Taylor had smiled though. Fox thought they were like, boyfriends now? He opened the door and felt a rush of excitement and nerves, distracted by the thought of it as he walked into the living room.

"Where the fuck have you been?"

Fox stopped and saw his mum at the sink. She looked pissed.

"Out. Kalum's," Fox waved his hand behind him.

"Kalum called," she said. Her smile was mean.

"Oh, yeah, well, you know. I went to Hayley's."

She walked over to the edge of the bench and cocked her hip against it, sizing him up. He felt small. It was fucking ridiculous – he was twenty years old, for fuck's sake.

"I can go out you know," he said.

She raised an eyebrow. "Of course you can, but you disappear for days, you think I'm not gonna wonder where you are? You think you shouldn't have to call?"

"You wonder where my money is you mean," he muttered.

"What did you say?"

Fox felt a rage come over him then. This impotence he'd felt for years, this tangle of shame and guilt and like he owed her something was drowned out by a rush of anger.

"I left you my pay, what more do you fucking want from me?"

She slapped him. It happened so quick, he barely knew what was happening.

"I'm your mother!"

He was still in shock from the slap. But, well, he had a lot to fucking say about that.

"Yeah? And what kind of mother fucking drains her kid's bank account?" he yelled.

He was looming over her and he hadn't even realised he'd moved.

"Go on, hit me. Hit me, you worthless little piece of shit. Go on, just like your fucking father."

Her eyes flashed with rage. He knew she wanted him to do it. She wasn't afraid at all. This is what she wanted – drama, something to cry martyr about. His dad wouldn't kill a mosquito, let alone hit her.

He hated the fucking cliché, but, "You're not fucking worth it," he said and walked off.

"Get back here," she screamed. Then, "Get out of this fucking house!"

"Fucking gladly!" he shouted and slammed his door. Locked it.

She was still yelling – how he was ungrateful, how he was lazy, just like his fucking father – and like, his dad was a regular guy who worked pretty hard; he didn't get it. But Fox looked like him. And he walked like him. And he was laid back like him. And that was enough for a lifetime charge of insolence.

"What the fuck is going on out here?"

Clarissa.

Then his mum's sobbing. He could hear her, "The way he talks to me. I just care where he is, I'm his mother!"

"Mum," Clarissa said and her voice was resigned, her sigh audible. Then she lowered it and all Fox could hear were murmurs.

His hands were shaking.

For a second there.

Yeah, he could've hit her.

He needed to get the fuck out of here. He grabbed his backpack and cast around for what he wanted. Jeans. Socks. Shirts. Boxers. He pulled out his Canning College application and looked at it. He shoved it back and slammed the drawer shut. He shouldered his bag, opened the window and popped out the flyscreen. He slipped out, shut the window and walked down the back, over the creek and onto the main road. He jogged along the tree line for a bit and then crossed when the traffic let up. He turned back and saw the bus coming and ran. The driver saw him and slowed.

"Thanks," Fox said as he hopped on. His chest was wheezing again. He paid for a full zone and went to the back seat.

Fuck. He didn't know where he was going.

Yes, he did.

Because if he wanted to go to Kalum's, he wouldn't have hopped the bus back down the hill. If he wanted to go to Kalum's or Hayley's, he would've walked up the road past the high school. He might not want to admit it, but he knew exactly where he was going.

13

B Y THE TIME HE was walking up Taylor's street – the apartment block a grey beacon of light ahead of him – Fox had second-guessed himself, talked himself out of it, told himself to go back, and asked what the fuck he thought he was doing. His feet just kept on moving. To the train station. To the city. To the bus station. To the next bus. To peering out into the darkness until he saw the shops he recognised. To here. The bottom of Taylor's steps.

Fox took a deep breath, shouldered the pack higher. Taylor's car was where he always parked it, so he was here at least. Maybe it'd be better if he wasn't. Then Fox would have an excuse to turn around, to just go... Somewhere else.

His feet marched up the steps. He stood outside Taylor's door. His hand shook. He squeezed it, released it, brought it up, and punched the door three times with his fist. Why'd he do it like that? He was such a fucking weirdo. There was the sound of footsteps inside. Fox caught the movement of the lace curtain over the sink, saw it flutter and fall back, and he swallowed hard.

The door opened.

"Fox?"

Taylor was surprised to see him. Fox could see it.

"Um, hey," he said and brought his hand up. He winced at himself and dropped his hand.

Taylor tilted his head and smiled, small. "Hey."

Fox thought he was going to cry.

Taylor stopped smiling and straightened. He moved back and opened the door wide. "Are you alright?"

Fox came inside, careful to keep out of Taylor's space – which was fucking stupid, he'd had his dick in his mouth – but he felt bad for being here.

"Sorry," he said and stopped at the bench.

"What for?"

Taylor was behind him and Fox wanted to turn and face him.

"For coming here."

"You can always come here."

And now Fox really thought he might cry. He hung his head and squeezed his eyes shut. Cleared his throat.

"Fox, what happened."

Taylor was still behind him. Fox shook his head. He couldn't get his voice to work.

"Here, can I," Taylor said and Fox felt him move closer, still careful not to touch. Then his hand was on the strap of Fox's backpack and Fox let him pull it off his shoulder, let him place it on the floor in front of the bench.

Fox turned, his head still down so his eyes were on Taylor's bare feet. He had really nice feet. Fox shuffled forward, and Taylor was still, and then Fox moved in without thinking and grabbed Taylor hard around the waist. Taylor met him, his hands coming up to envelope Fox in a hug, pulling him close to his chest. Fox felt Taylor's chest expand as he breathed in deep and he crushed Fox closer on the exhale. Fox pressed in more. His eyes were stinging but he didn't let it go any further. He wouldn't. He swallowed. Taylor's hand began a rhythm up and down his spine.

They stood like that for a long time.

"Sorry," Fox said as he pulled back.

He met Taylor's eyes.

"What happened."

"It's stupid," Fox replied and looked down.

Taylor brought his hand up, tentative; he lifted Fox's chin until his eyes were back on him.

"It's not."

"My mum," Fox's voice cracked.

Taylor exhaled, rough and relieved?

"What?"

Taylor brought his hand around the back of Fox's neck and rested it there.

"I thought, you know."

Fox shook his head. He really didn't.

Now Taylor looked shifty. Fox's heart started pounding.

"You regretted it or someone hurt you because of it or something," Taylor said.

Fox still had his arms loosely around Taylor's waist. He dug his fingers in when he realised what Taylor was saying. He felt even stupider.

"No," he huffed a laugh. "That'd make more sense, cos I'm all like this over nothing."

"Not nothing. She's your mum."

Fox dropped his head onto Taylor's shoulder and sighed. Taylor moved his hand again.

"Still fucking stupid."

"Why don't you tell me what happened and I'll tell you if it's stupid."

"You're not busy?"

Taylor shifted his head so his lips could press against the side of Fox's head, along his hairline.

"No."

So, Fox told him. Taylor got them beers and then sat next to him on the couch and listened. Fox hunched forward, eyes on the beer as he recounted the incident. It was such a non-event. God, he was a drama queen. No, he was too sensitive. Clarissa always said that to him, you're too sensitive.

"I'm too sensitive," he said as he finished.

Taylor hummed behind him. Their thighs were pressed together, but otherwise, Taylor had just sat, drinking his beer and listening.

"I dunno, I never had a mum. But. I hope I'm not out of line..."

Fox craned his head back. Taylor watched him, serious. "She sounds like a real bitch."

Fox laughed. His heart hurt too though.

"But she's still your mum," Taylor said.

So, he got it.

"And I still gotta live there," Fox sighed and sat back. Taylor let him press into him, his head on his shoulder.

"Well, you can stay here for a bit if you want."

Fox was embarrassed for himself, but his dick stirred at that.

"I've got a spare room," Taylor said.

And his dick might've misread the situation. He nodded, eyes down.

"Or, you don't have to, I mean, I can drive you to Kalum's."

Now Taylor sounded unsure. Which made Fox feel even more unsure.

"I can go there if you want, yeah. Sorry," Fox sat forward again.

"I don't want," Taylor said, quick.

Fox started thinking about bus timetables.

"Sorry," Taylor laughed, lightly disparaging himself. "I'm fucking this up."

"Fucking what up?" Fox asked.

"I want you to stay. In my room, if you want. But I don't wanna, you know."

Fox's heart fluttered and his dick stirred again.

"You don't wanna?"

He glanced back at Taylor. Cool, unflappable – everywhere they go girls salivate all over his dick Taylor – was sitting there looking unsure of himself.

"Presume."

Fox couldn't help it, he laughed.

"Think we passed that point when I sucked your dick, man."

Taylor laughed too, soft, shook his head. "Probably. Still."

"Still what?"

"I don't wanna like, pressure you."

"My dick gets hard every time you mention your room, man. No pressuring."

Fox felt a lick of shame as he said that, but Taylor slid his hand forward, over Fox's thigh and gripped his half-hard dick over his jeans, so he didn't really have time to dwell on it.

"Cool," was all Taylor said and he smiled, smug.

Fox laughed again, around the moan that wanted to come out when Taylor started to rub, and he felt like a chick in one of Clarissa's dumbass movies when he said, "Fuck. Bed, now."

14

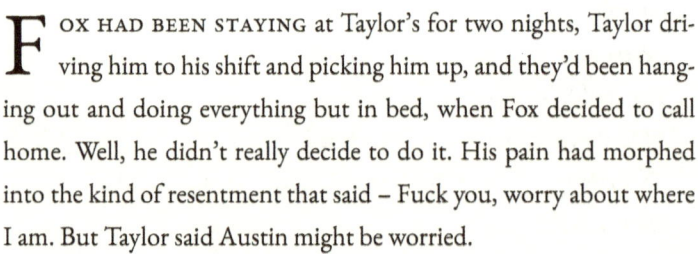

F OX HAD BEEN STAYING at Taylor's for two nights, Taylor driving him to his shift and picking him up, and they'd been hanging out and doing everything but in bed, when Fox decided to call home. Well, he didn't really decide to do it. His pain had morphed into the kind of resentment that said – Fuck you, worry about where I am. But Taylor said Austin might be worried.

Fox scoffed. "He doesn't worry," cos he didn't. Guy had one gear: chill.

Taylor shrugged, he ran his hand down Fox's back and kissed the back of his neck as he came around the kitchen bench.

"You'd be surprised," he said as he went to the sink, started rinsing their breakfast dishes. "Guys just don't show it."

"I do," Fox muttered. "Can I use the phone?"

"Don't have to ask." Taylor smiled at him in that soft way that got Fox every time. One side of his lips quirked up more than the other and his eyes crinkled. Fox mumbled thank you in an attempt to cover his feelings about it.

He went to the couch, flopped down and dialled home. His mum had a shift. Clarissa wouldn't be up yet. Austin should be home. It almost rang out.

Then, "'ello?"

"Hey."

"Hey," Austin's voice went up slightly. He was happy then.

"I'm at Taylor's."

"Cool."

"Yep."

He heard Austin moving around, knew he was moving to sit on the bench and angle the phone cord.

"Mum lost her shit, eh?"

"Yep."

Austin blew out a breath that sounded like a laugh. "Yeah. Gotta ignore her."

"I know."

"She's been calling all your friends."

Fox groaned.

"Clarissa says she had a synapse that remembered she was a mum."

Fox laughed.

"But you know she just wants everyone to think she is," Austin said.

Fox stopped laughing. He did know that. He didn't want to know that.

"She's probably forgotten by now though," Austin said.

"Cool."

"Did you watch *X-Files*?"

And Fox did. So they talked about that and then wound down and Fox said he'd probably come back at some point, to which Austin said, "Cool."

"All good?" Taylor asked after Fox had hung up and sat staring at nothing for a while.

"Yeah, she's forgotten about it."

Taylor was standing near him, showered and fully dressed. Right, he probably had somewhere to be. Like, in his life.

"She does that?" Taylor asked at the same time as Fox said, "I'll get out of your way."

"Huh?" Taylor said as Fox said, "What?"

"You go," Fox said.

"Oh, I just asked if she does that. Blows it all up on you and then forgets. Cos that's bullshit."

Fox liked how pissed off Taylor got about this. But he still had these conflicted feelings about it, so he just shrugged, said, "Yeah," and went to get his shit.

"And you're not in my way?"

"Yeah, but," Fox waved his hand up and down Taylor's clearly ready to leave attire.

"We've got a run," Taylor said. Then he smiled at Fox like he was endeared by his stupidity.

"Oh!"

"Yeah," Taylor grinned. "I'm ready whenever you are."

"I gotta shower," Fox said and rushed down the hall.

"Take your time," Taylor called and Fox heard him picking up the phone.

When Fox came out in clean jeans, black shirt, bare feet and wet hair, Taylor was still talking to someone on the phone. Or he was talking to someone else. Fox wondered if he should give him some privacy, but Taylor smiled at him, rolled his eyes and said to whoever it was, "It's two or it's never."

And, wow. Fox ducked his head at the tone. He couldn't help it. Taylor sounded authoritative, yeah, but mean too, harsh. Fox was hard-wired to cower and hide from a voice like that.

"Green shopping bag. Don't talk to us."

Fox heard the phone hang up.

"I don't usually like to do that over the phone, but..."

And the change in his tone was remarkable. Fox glanced up from tying his laces; Taylor looked apologetic. And he sounded ... Well, he sounded like he always did with Fox. Kind, open.

It was disorienting.

"Huh?"

"I don't like organising this shit over my phone, usually."

"So, why did you?"

Fox sat up and flicked his hair out of his face. It'd dry. Taylor walked over to him, his hips and beautiful dick at Fox's eyeline. Fox swallowed.

"Cos I've been busy," Taylor said and ran his hand through Fox's hair.

It felt nice, but, "Shit. Sorry."

Taylor tugged the strands and Fox leaned into it.

"Nothing to be sorry for," Taylor said. He was dragging his hand through Fox's hair and it reminded Fox of when he blew Taylor. How Taylor liked to get a good grip in his hair.

"Fuck, we gotta go," Taylor said but didn't move away.

"Okay."

Taylor leaned down and kissed him. Fox kissed back, his arms coming up to wrap around Taylor's shoulders until he was being yanked to his feet and crashing into Taylor's chest. It was a desperate kiss. Fox didn't really understand it, but he was all for it.

Taylor pulled back, his lips still so close they were sharing air.

"Sorry, but out there," he said and trailed off.

Fox was confused, he wanted more kissing. He leaned in and Taylor met him. It was getting heated and Fox was wondering if he could angle his hips just right –

Taylor pulled back. Then he gave Fox one more brutal kiss before stepping away entirely.

"Okay, later," he said and turned to start grabbing his shit.

Fox adjusted himself and then remembered what Taylor said.

"Out there what?" Fox asked, he sounded breathless.

Taylor waved his hand, he had his cigarettes in them.

"We can't, you know." He turned to look at Fox, and his expression was apologetic.

"Oh, yeah, of course." Fox nodded.

"That's okay?"

Fox thought about Tony. Kalum. His mum. Christ, anyone besides Austin and Clarissa and maybe Hayley knowing he was sucking dick and he had to stop the panic.

"Yeah," he said, gruff.

A pained expression flashed in Taylor's face, but then he smothered it, said, "Good," and headed for the door. Fox followed him out.

15

Fox hadn't thought he'd notice the space between them. But standing in the clubhouse, Tony and some other fucking clowns around, he not only felt it, he feared the alternative. They'd been in a real bubble the last few days, and if anyone ever saw that bubble, it wouldn't just burst, it'd get smashed to fucking smithereens.

"I got eight," Tony was saying. "You fob me off Monday, you can do eight."

Fox watched Taylor's jaw clench. Tony was a big fucker, but Taylor was taller and he was built and, as Fox knew intimately, cut. Taylor was also pretty fucking intimidating, he pulled off silent and dangerous like it was who he was, like it was all he was to these fuckers. But Tony carried the weight of this place. Fox hated even thinking it, but it gave him a gravitas that made the interaction tense. An almost match.

"We agreed on four."

"Well, now I need eight."

Fox heard a tittering from the bar and glanced over. Three goons were sitting there, listening, making no effort to hide their joy at the dressing down. That's how this place rolled. Like a demented pecking order where everyone was vying for a higher rung and terrified of holding their perch once they got there.

"I do eight, in one day, I want eighty percent."

Fox almost choked. He managed to hide it. He felt those assholes glance at him anyway.

Tony scoffed. "You might be my cousin, but don't get ahead of yourself. Fifty percent, like always. What the fuck were you doing you couldn't get this shit done Monday anyway?"

Tony turned away as he said it, like he was done with the conversation.

"Just went up to ninety."

The guys at the bar went quiet. Fox felt his skin skitter with nerves.

Tony looked back at him; his eyes glinted angrily, but there was something else there.

"Sixty."

"Eighty."

"Seventy."

"Seventy," Taylor nodded. "Be back later."

Taylor turned around. He met Fox's eyes with a cold look and nodded for the door. No one said anything to them as they left, but he heard Tony laughing and muttering, "Well, fuck me."

They walked in silence to Taylor's car, got in, and Fox stayed quiet. Taylor started the engine and spun out in reverse a little too fast, righted the car and sped back to the main road. They were a careful distance apart, like they had been since they stepped out the door, but Fox really felt it now, like that place and Taylor's standoff had chilled everything between them.

But then Taylor whistled and Fox glanced at him. Taylor was grinning.

"I was gonna try and get us sixty."

"You fucken planned that?"

"Yeah, course. Fucking fifty percent between us," Taylor shook his head in disgust and hit the indicator.

He peeled onto the highway, heading east.

"Wow," Fox shook his head in disbelief.

"You reckon we don't deserve seventy?" Taylor sounded like he really wanted to hear Fox's opinion.

"It's not that, I mean, I've never thought about it. But fuck, man. Tony's not someone I wanna even try that on."

Taylor shook his head. "Nah, I mean, you're right. He's a fucking unpredictable asshole, but one thing you should know about Tony. He wants someone to take it to him. He wants the challenger. In his own twisted way, he respects it."

"Probably helps that you're related," Fox said.

"Yeah, there's that. But," Taylor trailed off. Fox waited.

Fox lit a cigarette and handed it to Taylor who took it with a thanks and then Fox lit his own.

"It's not just that. I've seen other guys do it, when I was younger."

"For real?"

"Yeah, well. Most of them got their asses kicked, but this one dude, Māori guy? Man, he held his own," Taylor said. "Don't think he was gay, but."

Fox jerked at the comment and looked at Taylor. He was smiling. He met Fox's eyes and winked. They were stopped at a red light.

"You know, in case you were thinking about trading up."

Fox scoffed. "I don't think there's any further up," he replied without thinking.

Taylor's smile widened and then he looked back at the road when the light changed to green.

"Good, glad I impressed you, babe."

Fox felt his heart flutter. "Don't get ahead of yourself."

"Second person to tell me that today," Taylor took a drag, "and yet."

Fox felt himself blush for no reason. He was impressed. Taylor was so far out of his league it was ridiculous. He felt self-conscious about it. It also explained a few things, he realised as he took a drag and settled back in his seat, eyes on the suburb out the window. The further out they went, the shitter it looked – overgrown weeds, dilapidated houses, wire fences and the odd shipping container in a yard. Fox had always felt himself measuring himself against other guys. And yeah, all guys did that, but this had felt different. Like, he really noticed how hot and impossibly better than him some guys were and he'd obsess over it. Think about it. Watch it. Watch them. He never felt like that about a girl. He was comfortable around them. He'd put it down to having a sister. But that made no sense, and anyway, she was hardly someone who put anyone at ease. She made him feel safe, yeah, but not at ease. It was like having a snake as a protector – it'll strike anyone in walking distance, but it's gonna bite you too.

"You good?" Taylor asked.

Fox realised they were almost at the edge of the suburbs.

"Yeah," he said. "Just thinking."

Taylor drummed his fingers on the steering wheel. NIN's *Pretty Hate Machine* was low enough they could talk.

"I set a few of these up this morning, same as before," Taylor said. He sounded like he was trying to reassure Fox.

"Cool. The phone calls?"

"Yeah."

"Where'd you usually set it up. I mean, you said you didn't do it from home? If that's not, I mean, it's not my business."

Taylor's hand landed on his thigh and squeezed. "I trust you."

He took his hand back and explained how he normally did it at the servo near the clubhouse or used a payphone.

"Tony reckons I'm paranoid, but fucked if I'm going to prison for some pissy amount of money."

Fox reckoned going to prison for anything would suck balls. He said as much.

Taylor hummed. "There's some things worth going to prison for."

And that was ominous, but before Fox could ask, Taylor went on.

"What are you thinking about?"

"Huh?"

"Before, you said you were just thinking?"

Oh, right. Embarrassing. Fox shook his head and lit another cigarette. It tickled his throat and he held it up for Taylor. Taylor shook his head and Fox dragged.

"Just, you know, my sister and shit."

"Your sister?"

"Yeah, you know how your brain drifts? Like, you're in one thought and then you're in another one and it's just, I dunno, meandering. Nothing special."

Taylor nodded. "Yeah. Where'd you start then?"

Goddammit.

"Oh, you know, just about guys and shit."

He smoked and tried to sound unaffected. He was practically fucking Taylor, it's not like he wouldn't know Fox might be thinking about guys.

"And you ended up on your sister?"

Taylor was laughing at him. It was still so incongruous with the other Taylor. The one everyone else got. Fox loved it.

"Shut up," he smiled. "I told you, meandering."

Taylor nodded and turned left onto the highway out of the city.

"So," Taylor said, "guys, huh?"

Fox couldn't quite read his tone. Curious. Wary. Teasing.

Fox butted out the cigarette. He figured if you couldn't talk openly with the guy you were – fucking? dating? – then who could you tell?

"Yeah, just, you know. I'd always noticed or like, been into them, now I think about it. It was just, you know, unthinkable before."

Taylor nodded.

"Was it like," Fox paused, "for you?"

"Nah," Taylor shook his head as he pulled onto the left shoulder and headed down a gravel road. "I found Tony's dad's porn when I was a kid. I saw the guy's dick and knew I wanted it."

"Jesus," Fox huffed.

Taylor gave him a sly smile as he navigated the potholes pretty quickly. "Yeah. Fucked a few girls to be sure but yeah, nah."

"Are we going to someone's house?"

Taylor grinned at him, like he was allowing the subject change. "Yeah. This is the only one I'll make an exception for."

Fox was surprised. And curious.

They turned down a narrower lane and hit a gate. Taylor threw it in park, went to get out and Fox said he'd do it.

"Okay, make sure to refasten it after I'm through."

"Yeah, I know the drill, I grew up on a farm," Fox said as he got out.

He walked up to the fence, boots crunching in the whiter sand, and lifted the pole and brought the wire circle up and off and then walked it open in a wide arc. Taylor cruised through and Fox moved it back, lifted the wire back with some effort until it slipped over the pole, and went back to the car.

"I didn't know you grew up on a farm," Taylor said as he got back in. "Whereabouts?"

Fox told him the name of the nearest town that no one ever knew.

"No shit?"

"No shit," Fox said and didn't bother with the seatbelt.

"Hot," Taylor said.

Fox nodded. "Fucking freezing in winter though."

"Wheat and sheep?"

"Yep. Dad's still there."

"Huh," Taylor said.

"What?"

Taylor glanced at him just before they pulled up in front of a small farmhouse at the end of the road.

"Nothing. Just like, you know. Learning shit about you."

Fox dropped his head and shook it around a little smile. Did all guys just say nice shit like that?

"Same," he managed to mumble as Taylor killed the engine.

"Now, this guy's a bit weird, but he's cool. I've known him all my life."

"And he buys gear?"

"Yeah, but, he needs it."

With that, Taylor got out, told Fox to bring the bag.

Fox grabbed it and saw the flyscreen door bang open and an old guy emerge. He had a walking stick. And he was really fucking old.

"Taylor," he said, he was smiling.

"Jimmy."

Then this old man, Jimmy, noticed Fox and his face transformed into surly and pissed off.

"Who's your friend," he said.

"This is Fox, he's with me," Taylor said, but like he was saying something more.

"He's with you," the guy repeated, heavy.

"He's with me," Taylor said again.

The guy looked Fox up and down. He brought his hand up to his grey facial hair and scratched.

He hummed, like he was thinking.

"Not one of Tony's."

Fox screwed his face up, he couldn't help it.

"Nah," Taylor said. "He's all mine."

Fox thought that was an odd way of putting it. But it seemed to dissipate the tension cos the old guy huffed, "Yeah, alright," and opened the door wider.

Jimmy insisted on getting them tea and biscuits and sitting them down at the old table while he got his scales out. They looked like they were from the nineteenth century. Fox kept that thought to himself as he watched the old man take the bag, weigh it, and mutter about how much Tony was cutting the shit.

Fox sipped his tea and tried not to crack up at this old man who looked like one of the dads of the oldest farmers back home and yet he talked like a fucking gangster.

"Yeah, he says he's not, but you know," Taylor said and sipped his tea.

"Says he's not, that fat fucker," Jimmy replied and disappeared down the hall with the bag.

Taylor looked at Fox. Fox raised both eyebrows and Taylor looked like he was doing everything not to laugh.

"Whaddya two giggling about?"

Fox startled. For a guy with a cane and an old house, he moved quiet.

"Nothing. Tony," Taylor said.

"Fucking Tony," Jimmy said as he heaved himself into a seat and took a biscuit. "I always told ya, ya gotta get away from that fucker. He'll drag ya down, kid. He'll drag ya down."

Taylor nodded. "Just getting some cash together, then I'm out."

Jimmy nodded.

"What about you?"

He turned to look at Fox. His eyes were that milky colour old people had. Fox didn't like looking at it.

"Me?"

"Ah, it speaks," Jimmy said and sat back as he bit into his biscuit. Then he talked around it, "Seem like a good kid. And ya with Taylor here. Whaddya doing with this shit."

Fox shrugged. "Just getting some cash."

"What for?" He was peering at Fox with those eyes. Fox had the feeling he was a clever old fuck.

"Umm, you know, life," Fox said and lifted his tea cup. It was that old white kind, with painted roses on it. His nanna had had a set like this.

Jimmy smiled. It did not look nice.

"What's the deal with this one, Taylor," he said, eyes not leaving Fox's face.

Fox coughed, his chest rattling a bit, and Jimmy's eyes narrowed.

"Leave him alone, Jim," Taylor said and took another sip of his tea.

Taylor was sitting there, long legs crossed, looking relaxed and amused, while Fox squirmed under the third degree.

"He's too young," Jimmy said. "Fucking Tony," he went on and shook his head, looking away finally. "Going after little kids now. It's bad enough when it was you."

"I can handle myself."

"Now."

Fox saw Taylor's body go tense at that, but he just agreed and asked Jimmy how the dispute over the acacias was going and that set Jimmy off.

By the time they left, Fox had drunk too much tea, he needed to piss, and he was – embarrassingly – too scared to ask to use Jimmy's.

He was stoked to be getting out of that place. It was more unnerving than the average crack house. At least those people were out of it.

"I don't get it," he said as soon as Taylor had waved, Jimmy saluting him from the porch, and driven back up the dirt track.

"What's he need gear for?"

"He uses it," Taylor said like it was completely normal – nay, condonable – for eighty-plus-year olds to be using.

"But, he's so old."

"Yeah, so it makes sense doesn't it?" Taylor slowed down at the gate. "Makes more sense for an old dude who needs the kickstart to be on it than some eighteen-year-old tweaker."

Fox tilted his head and scrunched his face up. He got out to do the gate. Then he thought about where he could piss. He looked around. There were trees. He leaned the gate on the nearest tree and went to piss. Then he jogged back, did the fence, and jumped back in the car.

Taylor was smiling at him. "You could've used the toilet you know."

"That guy was fucking terrifying," Fox said as he put his seatbelt on.

Taylor laughed. "Jimmy? He's harmless."

Fox scoffed. "I wouldn't have been surprised if he came out onto the porch with a shotgun."

"He would've if it was Tony," Taylor said and smiled.

Fox didn't know if he was joking or not.

"Anyway, Jim's got real bad arthritis, it helps, apparently," Taylor said.

"How do you know him anyway?"

The trees were whipping by and Fox was watching them. Taylor didn't reply and Fox looked at him.

He was focused on the road, hands clenching and unclenching on the steering wheel.

"He's my grandfather," Taylor said.

Fox's mouth dropped open. "Fucking seriously?"

"Yep."

So, that meant, but Taylor beat him to the answer. "Not Tony's. Jimmy's my mum's dad. My dad and Tony's dad were brothers."

Fox was going to need a minute to wrap his head around the fact Taylor was selling gear to his grandfather. Was that badass? Or was that... What was that?

Taylor slowed at the turnoff back onto the highway. He didn't turn. He ran a hand through his hair. When he glanced at Fox, he looked unsure but determined. Fox braced himself for further cartel level family shenanigans.

"I wanted to like, have him meet you. Even though, you know," Taylor reached over and slipped his hand onto Fox's shoulder, brushing his fingers lightly on the bare skin above his collar, "he doesn't know."

Fox blew out a breath and leaned into the touch.

"Sorry I called him terrifying," was what his brain came up with. He winced at himself, but Taylor smiled.

"'S okay," he dug his fingers in and then let go. He returned his hand to the wheel, looked both ways and then pulled out. "He liked you."

"He liked me?"

"Course."

"That was him liking someone?"

Taylor laughed. "Yeah, man."

"I suddenly feel less nervous about you meeting my mum," Fox said and felt presumptuous and giddy, but Taylor smiled over at him, and said, "Yeah," and they went back into the city.

16

F OX FINISHED UP HIS shift, caught the bus home, walked in the front door, padded across the dark living area to his bedroom and found a note taped to his door in his mum's scrawl – *Taylor called, 11pm, call him back.*

It was dark except for the blue light streaming in through the kitchen window, lighting up the space near the phone and the little table. Quiet other than the sound of an occasional car on the main road. He dropped his bag at his door, went to the phone and picked it up and dragged it as far into the living room as the cord would allow and sat in front of the outside door. He dialled.

Then he thought about the time and wondered if Taylor meant, call him back at a reasonable hour tomorrow.

"Hello," came down the line in Taylor's gravelly voice before Fox could hang up.

"Hey, shit, sorry," Fox said.

He heard Taylor yawn and say, "What for?" around it.

"Waking you up."

"Was waiting for you to call, glad you got my message."

Fox could hear what sounded like movement on the other end of the line, like Taylor was moving around in his bed. Because Taylor had a phone in his room, Fox remembered.

"I got it," Fox said and pulled out his cigarettes. He cracked open the glass sliding door and lit one, blowing smoke out and looking up at the moon. The whole courtyard looked blue.

"You're quiet," Taylor said. Fox thought it sounded like he was sitting up, lighting a cigarette too.

"Everyone's asleep," Fox said.

Taylor blew out a breath. Fox imagined him exhaling his smoke, then scratching his bare chest as he woke up.

"Sorry," he said after a minute.

"Huh?" Fox said.

"For getting you to call."

"Nah," Fox replied and ashed his cigarette. "It's cool. Did you need anything?"

Taylor blew out another breath. "Nah, just wanted to say hi, see how your shift went."

"Oh, you know, same old shit."

Taylor hummed. "Yeah, but at least it's legal I guess."

"I guess."

Fox didn't know where this was going, but he realised he was happy. Talking to Taylor. Having it be the last thing he did in the day, it was nice.

"Was Tony pissed we didn't move all eight?"

"Nah, man," Taylor laughed, it still sounded gravelly, "I sold em."
"Yeah?"

Taylor had said, "I'll take care of it," but Fox hadn't thought he'd meant tonight.

"Course. I got your cut."

"Don't pay me for the ones you did this time, alright? It doesn't feel right."

"Fox?"

His mum's voice drifted into the living room. She came closer and stopped at the threshold to the room. Fox could see the white of her dressing gown, her face like a black shadow.

"Hang on," he said to Taylor and brought the receiver to his chest. "Yeah?" he asked her.

"Taylor?" she said and he couldn't see her expression, but her head moved, nodding at the phone.

"Yeah."

She nodded again. "Well, don't stay up too late."

And then she walked out. He could hear her footsteps moving on the carpet, then the tiles of the entryway, and then she was closing her bedroom door.

Fox exhaled.

"Hey," he said as he brought the phone back up.

"Your mum?"

"Yeah."

"I spoke to her before, when I called."

"Whaddya mean spoke to her?"

"Just, you know, she answered the phone."

Fox lit another cigarette and slid the door open more. He wished he grabbed a beer before he sat down.

"And I said to let you know I called, to call me back and she was like, 'Taylor,'" he started imitating Fox's mum's voice and Fox snickered, "'Fox's been staying with you hasn't he. I hope that hasn't been a problem.'"

Fox giggled. Taylor laughed with him.

"So, I said, 'Not at all, Fox is a perfect guest.'"

"And what'd she say?"

"I can't remember, but she sounded like, really proud, like she'd raised you right."

"Sounds about right," Fox said. He had this uncomfortable feeling now. It was familiar. She acted one way with him, and another with everyone else. It meant everyone thought he was full of shit about her. But then she was nice sometimes. Like tonight. That was her way of saying she was glad he was home.

"I know the play, Fox," Taylor said after a minute.

"What play?"

"Your mum. Tony can be the same. Cept he's more of an asshole most of the time, but yeah, you should see him with the family, if I told any of em what he was up to, they'd be like, 'Taylor, stop trying to get your cousin in trouble, tsk, tsk,'" he finished in another imitation of an old lady and Fox laughed.

"Yeah?"

"Yeah, man. Fucking assholes."

Fox agreed, but, "Yeah, I know, but."

"She's your mum."

"Yeah."

Fox was embarrassed by it. Austin didn't have this problem and Clarissa operated with it on another plane, but he did. He really was too sensitive.

"What're you doing tomorrow?" Taylor asked.

"Um, Kalum's having a thing."

"Cool."

"Did you wanna, maybe, the day after?"

Fox crushed his cigarette on the patio and wished he could articulate an invitation properly.

"Yeah, and um," Taylor said and breathed out, he sounded nervous. It made Fox feel nervous.

"I was thinking, and you can say no, obviously, but um, I've got this, well, Jimmy's got this friend who's got these cabins in Denmark, and it's free, and I was thinking of heading down for the weekend. Maybe taking some pot, beers, you know."

"Just us?"

"Well, yeah."

"Fuck yeah."

"Yeah?"

"Course. Oh, wait."

"What?"

"Work, but um, I'll call in sick."

"You sure?"

"Fuck yeah, man. I love Denmark."

Taylor laughed. "Cool."

Fox shook his head at himself and smiled; he did love Denmark, but they both knew that wasn't why he was saying yes.

"Pick you up Friday, early, say, six?"

"Sounds good."

"Good."

Fox could hear Taylor smiling as he said it.

"Well, I'll let you get some sleep," Taylor said. "Do you want me to drop your cut off tomorrow or?"

"Nah, I'll get it Friday. Only my part."

"Yeah, yeah, alright. Night, Fox."

"Night, Taylor."

Fox and Kalum had been playing for a few hours, drinking beers, and Kalum's shiftiness had gone from making Fox nervous to pissing him off.

Fox paused the game.

"What're you doing? I was about to finish the level," Kalum said, but he didn't sound all that invested. Which was weird as fuck.

"What's with you?"

"Whaddya mean?"

And even that sounded shifty.

"You know what I mean."

Fox sat forward, eyes on the screen. His heart was hammering, but he reckoned if Kalum knew, if he even suspected; well then, Fox wasn't sure what he was going to do. He hoped it'd be cool. He never thought he'd be here, in this position. Wondering if his best friend might have a problem with him liking guys. Well, a guy. He had no idea how to handle it.

Kalum sighed, deep and profound and when Fox glanced at him, he looked nervous.

Then he rushed out, "I hooked up with Hayley."

"What?"

Fox was so disoriented by the name and the information, he thought he misheard.

"We were drunk and I didn't mean to and I'll leave it at that if you want, but um, I really fucking like her, man. But I won't go there if, you know."

Fox frowned and then laughed.

"Go for it, man," he said around a laugh. "Hayley's awesome."

"You're not pissed?"

"No?"

Should he be?

Kalum grinned. "Yeah?"

"Yeah, man. That's awesome."

"Awesome."

They kept playing, the tension gone from the room. Fox was still wired, thinking he'd almost had to deal with the other secret between them, but he figured Kalum's general obliviousness was working in his favour.

So he was caught off guard when Hayley came round and the two of them were like an awkward couple around Fox and she said, "How's Taylor?"

And Kalum smiled, that big idiotic grin he got sometimes, and said, "Hey, yeah, you guys been hanging out a lot, eh?"

"He's good."

Fox sipped his beer.

"I still think he's a bit old," Hayley said.

"He's three years older than us," Fox said.

"That's a lot at this age."

"Geez, it's not like Fox's boning him," Kalum laughed.

Fox froze, his hand reaching to put his beer down. He saw Hayley see it and her face contorted. Fox couldn't make his mouth move to deny it. Kalum noticed the silence and didn't get it.

"What?"

"Nothing," Fox said.

Kalum was frowning now, and Fox could see the gears turning. He looked at Hayley, who was politely trying to cover her reaction. Then Kalum looked at Fox.

Fox brought his beer up and sipped it. He sat back and tried to look casual.

"Wait," Kalum said.

"Wait, what?" Fox hoped his voice sounded normal.

"You're not gay," Kalum said.

Fox didn't know what to say. He was glad he was drunk. Not shitfaced, but drunk enough that he wasn't having a panic attack. He sat forward again, put the beer down and ran a hand through his hair as he looked at the ground.

"But what if I am," Fox heard himself say.

He chanced a look up through his hair and Kalum's mouth was open and his eyes were bugging out.

"I'm gonna go," Fox said and stood.

Kalum stood as well. Fox was taller. And broader. But Kalum was scrappy. If it was gonna be a fight, it'd be messy. Fox braced himself for it. Kalum reached his hand out and Fox stepped back, instinctively. Kalum's hand dropped and he gaped at Fox.

"Fox, what? D'ya think I care?"

Fox looked up. Hurt and confusion warred on Kalum's face.

Fox shrugged. "Not like we know any gays and we always, you know."

"Always what?"

"Run em down," Fox shrugged again.

"Yeah, but like, not them, them. Shit, I just can't believe. Fox!"

Fox watched Kalum's face morph from shocked to hurt to angry and then he was coming in again, but Fox read it right this time and let Kalum pick him up in a big hug. Fox gripped him back, tight.

"I can't believe you thought I'd care," Kalum said against his neck and squeezed him hard.

Kalum pulled away and slapped Fox's back, then he got a sly look on his face.

"What?" Fox asked.

"Taylor?"

Fox ducked his head and blushed.

"Fucken nice, man."

"Kalum," Hayley said, surprised but indulgent.

"What? He's fucken hot. I'd do that if I you know, if I was like, you know."

Kalum ran his hand through his hair and smiled, sheepish.

"If you sucked dick?" Fox asked.

Kalum twisted his face up, blushed and then rushed out, "Not that there's anything wrong with that!"

Fox laughed. "I'm just fucking with ya."

Kalum blew out a breath. "Good, fuck. I need a beer."

"Me too."

Kalum got them a round and they put on some music, drank and listened to Hayley complain about everyone who'd been at the pub the night before. It was nice. Kalum shot Fox a few looks every now and then, but Fox reckoned he was checking in, saying – hey, we still cool? And Fox would smile at him as if to say – yeah, man, we're always cool.

He told Kalum as he left that he was going to Denmark for the weekend with Taylor and Kalum opened his mouth to say something, closed it, and then cracked up.

"What?"

"Sorry, it's like. Normally I'd say, you know, get it or whatever, but like, Taylor's the one who gets it, right?"

"Kalum!" Hayley hit him in the chest from where she was tucked under his arm.

Fox blushed and maybe because he was buzzed, he found that embarrassing rather than mortifying and why he said, "We switch out."

That shut Kalum up, like he was trying to work it out, so Fox said, "Later, man. Hayley," and headed out.

18

♥

FOX HAD HIS BACKPACK ready in the entryway, a carton of beer under it, a few packets of smokes stuffed in the top, and a bag of snacks. He went to the kitchen to get a coffee. Then he stopped. Maybe he didn't need another coffee. He glanced at the clock. Ten to six. He should just head up the driveway and wait.

The front door crashed open and Clarissa and Daria tumbled through it.

"Foxy!" Daria shrieked as she came into the room.

So, they were shitfaced again. Fox wondered how Clarissa managed it. She didn't work, she said it would interfere with her creativity, and yet she got high and drunk Wednesday through Sunday on Daria's paycheck and their mum's handouts. If he was Daria, and he worked the fucking meat counter at the shops, he'd tell Clarissa to get a fucking job.

"Oh, that's right," Clarissa said as she came in and slumped at the kitchen bench next to Daria who was lighting a cigarette and passing it back to her, "got your romantic weekend getaway," she finished as she took the smoke, had a drag, and blew smoke in his face.

"Shut up."

Fox decided it was a firm no on the coffee. He went back for his shit.

"We'll help you," Clarissa said.

Clarissa never helped anyone. She was either drunker than usual – probably not possible – or she wanted to embarrass him.

"I got it."

"We can help," Daria said and ashed her cigarette on the floor – God. Lucky their mum wasn't there; she already hated Daria on account of the Asian thing, so anything else was a bonus.

Clarissa was shouldering the backpack and Daria was picking up the shopping bag full of snacks and then Austin walked in and said, "Hey, heading out?" and picked up the carton.

Fox didn't know what else he could do, so he followed them up the driveway.

He heard Taylor's car before he saw it. And he could just imagine Taylor's surprised face when Fox's entourage crested the top of the driveway with all his shit. Clarissa was bitching about, "What the fuck is in here?" while Daria was saying, "Twisties! Fuck, we should get some Twisties, Clo," and Austin was thankfully saying nothing as he carried the carton on his shoulder.

Fox came up last and saw Taylor getting out. He was smiling. And Fox was not a romantic or a fucking poet, but damn, Taylor looked good in that crisp morning light. Casual jeans, loose black shirt, hair mussed, eyes crinkling with his smile.

"Hey," he said, a little surprised, a lot pleased. Damn, but Fox loved him. He blushed at the thought and looked away.

"Hey, man," Austin said. "Back seat?"

"Boot," Clarissa decided before Taylor could answer and Daria finished, "They might need the back seat."

They started laughing and Fox wanted to die. But Taylor was still smiling, looking between them, and Austin was rolling his eyes and going for the boot.

Clarissa dramatically threw the bag in next to the carton and Daria took the shopping bag to the front passenger seat and then Fox remembered the cigarettes. He went to the boot.

"What are you doing?" Clarissa asked.

"Smokes."

He poked around for them and she saw the packets.

"Can I have a pack? Pleeeaasse!"

"Fuck, no. Get your own."

"I got some," Taylor said.

"See, he's got some." Clarissa took a packet.

Fox grabbed the hood of the boot and went to slam it on her hand; of course, he wouldn't, but she shrieked and ducked away and then laughed.

"Have fun," Austin said and nodded at Taylor before walking off.

"Byee!!!" Clarissa and Daria said and thankfully said nothing else as they skipped down the driveway.

"Send off?" Taylor grinned.

"Fuckers," Fox replied as he went around for the passenger seat and got in.

Taylor got in and Fox said, "They just wanna gawk at you."

Taylor grinned. "That's alright with me. Hope I measure up."

"Pfft, they wish they could lock this down."

And it was too early and Fox's brain wasn't working well enough to filter well, that.

But Taylor smiled, soft, and hummed. He leaned over the dash and gave Fox a quick kiss.

"Hi."

"Hi."

"Alright," Taylor said and pulled back. "Denmark."

"Denmark," Fox replied. He could still feel that kiss on his lips. He hadn't touched Taylor for two days, and now they had a six hour drive before he could.

He sighed, sat back and saw his mum's car coming down the hill. His heart kicked up double time in a nanosecond. There's no way she saw that, but just the thought of it. Taylor cruised past her, slow, and she peered in. Fox waved. His mum didn't acknowledge him.

Fucking hell.

Fox blew out a tense breath.

Taylor turned left and the Valiant dropped down the descent. He didn't say anything, just gave Fox a quick glance. Taylor wasn't stupid – he'd feel the tension. Fox wanted to explain. He wasn't ashamed. Was he? No. He might be newly awakened to his love of dick, but he wasn't ashamed of what he did with Taylor, what he felt for him. Taylor was beautiful.

No. It was the fucking drama. Nothing could just be. She'd hit the fucking roof. And then there was the clubhouse and all those fucking jokers. Fox didn't know how him and Taylor were gonna do this.

They were turning onto the highway, Taylor fiddling with the stereo, shuffling CDs before settling on Creedence.

Fox snorted. "Really?"

"Creedence are fucking classic," Taylor said. He sounded relieved that Fox was talking to him. God. He was such a fucking drama queen.

"Sorry," he said and sat up.

"'S cool," Taylor said.

Fox was glad Taylor didn't pretend it was nothing. He acknowledged the presence of something in the car but didn't push it. And Fox didn't want to get into it.

"Creedence are big back home," Fox said.

"Yeah?"

"Yeah, gets played at music nights at the hall. I like it, just wasn't expecting it."

"You're lucky then," Taylor said. "We got The Eagles."

"No."

Taylor smiled. "Yes. But we got Guns N' Roses too. And The Doors."

"Yeah, same. Guns were big."

Taylor told him about Tony's love of The Eagles and how much shit he gave Taylor when he brought home *Use Your Illusion*. Fox laughed. No way was Tony letting anyone know that shit now.

Taylor cruised onto the highway out of the city and the suburbs quickly gave way to trees, the drag of the sixty and seventy zones pushing out to a hundred and ten and then the trees fell away and the paddocks whipped by as the Valiant held the bitumen close, dipped and barely rose as they flew down the single carriageway. Fox looked at Taylor, one hand on the wheel, the other one resting easy on the armrest on the centre console, his hand tapping to the beat of "Have You Ever Seen the Rain."

Fox rested his hand on top of Taylor's on the armrest and laced their fingers together. Taylor shot him a smile, surprised, and squeezed Fox's hand.

Fox sang the chorus softly.

And Taylor joined in.

They'd be alright, Fox thought and focused on the road.

19

♥

THE DIRT TRACK THEY pulled onto was before the town proper. Taylor said the old guy, the friend of Jimmy's, Vernon, rented the cabins here.

"They're not much, but that makes em kinda cool," Taylor said as he navigated around the potholes.

Two dogs ran out to greet the car.

"Greyhounds?" Fox asked. Little greyhounds.

"Whippets," Taylor said. "Sadie and Maggie."

The dogs drew up next to the car and then trotted along beside it like an escort.

"Vern accidently ran Maggie there over with his tractor last year," Taylor said and nodded to the white one on Fox's left.

"Fuck."

"Yeah," Taylor nodded. "Vern rushed her to Albany. She had to have a few surgeries. Alright now, but."

"She looks good," Fox said.

She did. Sleek, good runner.

"Yeah, she's a good dog."

"You want a dog, don't you?" Fox asked.

"Fuck yeah, but you know," Taylor replied as he stopped in front of a big farmhouse.

"Yeah, same," Fox said.

Gotta get your own place first. They'd had a dog. Their mum left it chained to a washing line when they left one of their many rentals. Said she'd organised someone to come pick it up. Took Austin telling him deadpan one day after Fox wondered out loud how Stimpy was doing that "No one was coming for that fucking dog."

And he didn't wanna think about that right now.

A skinny old guy was coming out of the main house, not smiling, but something about him seemed happy to see Taylor nonetheless. Taylor put it in park and got out.

"Taylor."

"Vernon."

Taylor leaned his arm on the top of the Valiant and Fox got out and did the same.

"This is Fox."

"Fox," Vern acknowledged him.

Maggie sniffed Fox's leg and he leaned down to pat her.

"Got you the far cabin. No one else here, but. If you want something else," Vern said as he rolled a cigarette.

He'd come down the steps and was leaning on the railing. Maggie wandered over to him and sat on his foot.

"Far cabin's good," Taylor said.

Vern licked his rollie and tightened it between his fingers, pressed it between his lips and lit it. He blew out the smoke and looked at Taylor. He had that long, easy gaze country people seemed to get. Like they were used to just looking at shit for a long time and didn't get all twitchy doing it. Fox's dad could do that. Fox's dad did it in a friendly way though. There was something impenetrable about Vern.

Something more like the rest of the country guys. Yeah, they'd move heaven and earth to save their dogs, but they'd sooner piss on anyone else than save them if they were bleeding on their land.

"No funny business," Vern said.

Fox tried not to twitch. The other dog, Sadie, came over, and he leaned down to give her a pat.

But Taylor just huffed a laugh, said he had his stuff and they'd let him know before they left that they were leaving.

Vern accepted that with a grunt and a "Later."

They got back in and followed a narrow road winding through massive old growth forest, glimpses of the ocean behind it. Right there.

"The beach is right fucking there," Fox said.

"Yep," Taylor replied.

"What'd he mean no funny business?"

Fox didn't want to ask, but well, he was suffering from severe blue balls being stuck in a car with Taylor all day and not getting off. So, if that was off the table, then fuck the beach and the forest and the secluded cabin. He'd take Taylor's dick in his mouth and vice versa in a filthy toilet block at this point.

"Drugs, gear," Taylor said and gave him a knowing and desperate smile, which made Fox feel better. "Nobody would even think the other thing."

And, well, Taylor was right. Cos Fox wouldn't have before. And the more he thought about it, the more he realised not only was being gay something no one ever talked about – other than the usual gay shit as insults – but no one even thought about it. It was a non-reality, a non-possibility.

Taylor stopped at a rickety shack that was, indeed, far from the main house. It was flanked by the beach behind it and the trees in front, the paint peeling, the stairs ancient, a perfect square that Fox imagined contained four rooms of the same size. He could see the toilet to the side.

Taylor got out and Fox went to go to the boot when Taylor said, "Inside first," and jogged up the stairs and pulled a key out of the meter box on the wall.

Fox followed him up, and Taylor opened the door, pushing it wide to allow Fox to step into the dim room. He felt Taylor crowd up behind him, heard the door kick shut, and Fox turned at the same time as Taylor's hand came down on his waist and spun him. Fox met his mouth and pushed him back against the door. Taylor pulled him in, and they were kissing, grinding, and both trying to unbuckle the other's pants with impatient fingers. Taylor got there first, and Fox's dick was wrapped in those skilled fingers. He gasped and redoubled his efforts to get to Taylor's dick. He got Taylor's belt undone, his fly buttons popped, and he slid his hand inside and felt Taylor's groan against his lips. They jerked each other off like that – quick and frantic with a sexual energy Fox was alarmed by. He came first – his mouth breaking away from Taylor's as he gasped while Taylor chased his lips, his kisses fierce as Fox tightened his grip and jerked him roughly. Taylor grunted and came, slumped back against the door, and brought Fox with him.

"Sorry," Taylor said after they'd caught their breaths, their kisses slowing, their hands resting on one another's junk.

"What for?"

"Jumping you."

Fox laughed. "I was gonna suggest we fuck in the first road-house toilets. You showed restraint."

Taylor laugh-smiled into Fox's throat before pulling his hand free, showing Fox to the bathroom to clean up.

Now that he'd taken the edge off, Fox could look around. It was four square rooms – kitchen, a living area with a fireplace, and two bedrooms with queen-size beds. The bathroom was a pokey thing at the back with a laundry. The furniture was old and used, and the whole place wore the battering of time and the ocean. But it was cosy. Fox could live here. He said as much.

"Fuck, man, I know. Same," Taylor said as he wiped his clean hands on his jeans.

There were no towels. Taylor said he brought some, and sheets and blankets and food to cook and all sorts of stuff Fox didn't even think of.

"I just brought beer and smokes," Fox said.

"And this is why I love you," Taylor told him with a wink, and then seemed to realise what he'd said and looked away, focused on pulling shit out of the boot as he mumbled, "You know what I mean."

Fox's heart was thumping, but he said, "Yeah, 's cool, I get it."

Taylor nodded, started handing shit to Fox and told him to chuck it all in the room with the bigger bed. Fox hadn't noticed a bigger bed, but he'd figure it out.

Taylor was shouldering Fox's backpack, and then the carton, a shopping bag in his other hand and following Fox up the stairs as Fox poked his head into the first bedroom.

"Next one," Taylor said. Well, grunted. Fox heard all the shit being put down while he went into the next room. It was bigger – the bed – one of those old, iron cast beds with fancy posts.

He threw the bedding on it and Taylor cleared his throat behind him.

Fox looked up and met his eyes.

"We don't have to share, if like, you want –"

"Oh, no. Well. I want, but if you –"

Taylor smiled, it was relieved but also, sly, sexy.

"Cool."

"Cool," Fox returned the smile and shook his head at himself as he turned and made the bed.

He was gonna need a beer. He went out and Taylor was already on it, handing him a bottle before he had to ask. The waves were crashing behind them, the trees whistling on all sides, and otherwise, silence. Fox sipped his beer and was about to suggest they head out when Taylor grabbed the wrist of his free hand and pulled him in for a kiss.

And alright, Fox thought, as Taylor led him to the couch and blew him, swapping blowjobs was a good idea too.

They made it to the beach later, after Taylor had cooked up steaks and served it with salad and fresh bread, and more beers, and a joint. Fox grabbed Taylor's hand in the darkness and stood on the shoreline, the water lapping his bare feet and legs where his jeans were rolled up. The booze made him feel loose, the pot horny, and Taylor's hand and quiet presence content and nervous all at once.

Taylor pulled him close and wrapped him up, his chin resting on Fox's shoulder while he watched the water that looked black in the night.

"You know I didn't bring you here just to fuck you, right?"

Taylor's breath tickled his neck as he spoke. Fox nodded.

"Yeah, I know. But we're gonna."

"Only if you want."

Fox did want, he was just stupidly scared. Of a dick, going up his ass.

"You can fuck me if you want," Taylor said, easy as anything.

Fox startled and craned his head back to look at him. He was close, and his eyes looked sleepy; he had big eyes and they were warm if he liked you.

"You don't wanna fuck me?"

Taylor huffed a laugh at Fox's throat and breathed, "Oh yeah, I do. But might be better for you, first time."

Fox turned back to face the water. He felt like a child, like he should be able to make himself do this, take it; it was Taylor, his whatever, boyfriend probably, it'd be fine.

"I don't mind," Fox said, which was a lie.

Taylor kissed his throat. "I do."

"You mind?"

"I mind if you like it. Plus, I've always wanted to try it."

"Yeah?"

"Yeah."

Taylor pulled away then, hand still laced with Fox's. "Maybe tomorrow."

"Not now?"

"You wanna go now?" Taylor sounded surprised. And a lot more awake.

Fox's dick was half hard from the conversation.

"Only if you want."

Taylor kissed him, then said, "I want."

They went back inside and instead of getting straight into bed, Taylor pulled out another beer each and lit a cigarette. He didn't look so tired anymore and Fox was feeling fucking wired. He took the beer though, followed Taylor to the living room.

Taylor pulled out a deck of cards. Fox laughed. "Really?"

"Strip poker. No touching," Taylor said and placed his cigarette in his mouth while he started to shuffle.

"Oh, it's fucking on," Fox said. Then he had to tell Taylor he'd never played.

"Never?"

"Nah, man. Who would I play poker with?"

Taylor maybe didn't know what him and Kalum got up to, which was gaming.

"Fair enough. Alright, it's easy."

Taylor shuffled and dealt and talked. Fox liked the way his mind worked. Careful, methodical; like he'd thought about each step as it built on the next one as he did things, and he explained it like that.

Fox took a swig of his beer, picked up his cards, and frowned.

"You'd make a good teacher," Fox said.

"And you'd make a shit poker player."

"What? Why?" Fox looked up in disbelief – he hadn't even done any playing yet.

"Your face," Taylor nodded at him, smirked. "Shitty cards?"

"Maybe I'm tricking you," Fox said and recrossed his legs.

He was sitting on the floor in front of the coffee table, Taylor across from him on the couch.

Taylor snorted. "Yeah, okay, Houdini. I'm the dealer. You need another card? You say hit me."

Fox nodded and made his face look thoughtful.

Taylor snickered. Fox rolled his eyes at him. "Hit me."

Taylor pulled a card from the top of the deck and slid it over to him. Fox picked it up. Ace. He smiled.

Taylor laughed.

"You wanna keep going?"

"You gonna fold?"

Taylor laughed again. "No fucking way I'm folding on this one."

"Alright," Fox said.

"Alright?"

"Yeah, let's go," Fox spread his cards out. Twos, fours, and his ace.

Taylor cracked up and spread his full house.

Fox shrugged, sheepish, and took a swig of beer.

"Shirt," Taylor said when he'd recovered.

Fox blushed, but took it off. It wasn't that cold in the room and even sitting hunched, he knew he looked alright. Not Taylor levels of hotness, which gave him some incentive to actually win a hand.

He picked up his new hand and kept his face blank.

"Good," Taylor said, he was nodding and looking at his cards.

Fox hummed. This was, in his less than ten minutes of experience, another shitty hand. He threw a card and called for another one anyway. Taylor dealt it. Fox drummed his fingers on the table.

Taylor got himself another card and sat back, legs sprawled. Fox glanced at his bulge and then back at his cards.

Taylor cleared his throat. "Hold em?"

"Yeah," Fox said after a minute.

"Alright," Taylor laid out a shitty hand as far as Fox could see.

Fox laid his cards out. Taylor had a slightly less shit hand. He smirked at Fox and said, "Pants."

Fox stood and undid his jeans, shimmied them down his thighs and legs, and kicked them off.

"I probably shoulda put more clothes on," Fox said as he sat back down in his boxers.

Taylor hummed. "Nah," he said and adjusted himself. Fox smirked. Taylor told him to shut up.

Fox wasn't smirking when he lost again.

"Um," he said and looked up. Taylor was looking back.

Fox shrugged and stood again. He went for his waistband and then reached for his beer, chugged it all down, and then shoved his boxers off. He was half hard from all the eye fucking and his dick kind of bobbed out as he sat back down.

He looked up and saw Taylor watching him, and he said, "What're we gonna do if I keep losing?"

Taylor looked back up to his face, he looked like he was trying to smirk, but it was lost in the way his voice went husky, "Might have to change the rules."

"You gonna get naked for me?"

Taylor shook his head. "Nah, not that rule. Touching. Might have to get some favours out of you."

Fox swallowed. "Deal then."

Fox, miraculously, won a hand and Taylor took his shirt off. Fox felt marginally better, although all that skin wasn't helping his dick go soft.

Taylor dealt the next hand quickly and won.

Fox huffed a laugh, nervous. He wanted another beer, but he didn't want to walk around naked.

"C'mere," Taylor said.

Fox stood and walked over to the couch. Taylor was still sitting back, but he ran his hands up the back of Fox's thighs, his eyes up on Fox's. Fox's breath caught. Taylor leaned in, eyes still fixed on Fox's face as he drew Fox closer with his palms cupping his bare ass, his lips pressing softly into the cut of his hip. Fox's lips parted and he watched as Taylor kissed across his abdomen, just above where his dick was straining upwards, careful to miss it.

Taylor massaged his ass, and Fox gasped. "Fuck, please."

Taylor's fingers dipped lower to stroke Fox's taint, dragging lightly over his balls. Fox brought his hands down to rest on Taylor's shoulders as he panted. Taylor took his dick into his mouth so suddenly, Fox almost bucked. Taylor gripped his hips tight as he sucked. He pulled off just as suddenly.

"I win," he said.

"What? Fuck, don't stop."

"You don't wanna play anymore? Get me naked?" Taylor asked as he clenched and unclenched his grip on Fox's ass.

"I'll get you fucking naked," Fox said and straddled Taylor's lap and kissed him.

Taylor met him, all bravado gone. Fox got his hands down that gorgeous chest, straight into his pants with frantic fingers. Taylor lifted his hips and let Fox push them down and off until they were both naked and Fox was coming back up to take his mouth again.

Taylor broke away and said, "Bed?"

"I need to get off," Fox said and kissed him again, grinding his dick against Taylor's.

Taylor groaned, but then broke off, again.

"You don't wanna fuck me?"

"Next round. I won't last," Fox said and Taylor groaned and kissed him hard for that.

Taylor reached between them and stroked them off rough and quick, and Fox did come embarrassingly fast, but Taylor wasn't far behind, so he wasn't gonna lose sleep over it.

"Shit," Fox said as they came down, Taylor's hand rubbing up and down his back.

"What?"

"I'm a shit poker player."

Taylor laughed. "Nah. Well, yeah, you are. But it's your first time, so."

Taylor kissed his collarbone and Fox rocked his hips. They were sticky and disgusting, but Fox was getting horny again anyway.

"Bed?" he asked.

Taylor kissed his throat. "Yeah."

Fox ground into him and Taylor kissed under his ear. "Go. I don't wanna fuck on this couch."

Fox felt his heart hammer at that and extricated himself. Taylor was right behind him. Fox went into the bedroom and pulled the covers back, and Taylor wasn't behind him. Fox lay down, his hand idly stroking his dick when Taylor walked in. He had a small wet towel in his hand, and he came over slowly, wiping himself down, before leaning over and doing the same to Fox with gentle movements. It was dialling Fox right up again. He panted and watched Taylor's face. The lamp was on, and Taylor's eyes were on the cloth cleaning Fox's skin. Taylor looked up, and Fox met his eyes. Taylor blinked slowly, his breathing a little shallow, his dark hair falling around his face. He looked aroused but tentative too. Fox brought his hand up and stroked his palm down the arm Taylor had braced on the bed near Fox's hip. Fox ran his hand up and down, the other one still idly stroking himself.

Taylor took him in and then breathed out, "Fuck, you're gorgeous."

Fox keened at that and felt embarrassed for it, but Taylor was blanketing his body and kissing him and he was too turned on to care.

Taylor pulled back after a moment, his hand roaming down Fox's chest to slide around his dick and stroke him. Fox bucked up into it, and Taylor slowed his movements. Fox groaned. Taylor chuckled and looked away from where he'd been stroking him to meet Fox's eyes.

"Nice dick," Taylor said. Fox thought from anyone else that would sound insulting or casual, but Taylor said it like he really thought Fox had a nice dick. Fox liked his dick – it was thick and long enough, he couldn't complain.

Taylor was still sliding his hand up and down, too slowly, and Fox breathed, "Thanks?" a question as he tried to get more.

"You can't come," Taylor said.

Fox had a moment of panic quickly followed by anger – he was going to kill Taylor if he kept jerking him like this.

Taylor moved up his body and kissed him, his lips still close as he said, "You're gonna fuck me."

Fox nodded. "Yeah."

Taylor let him go and stretched over the bed to reach into his bag. His body was a heavy weight on top of Fox's and Fox ran his palms up and down Taylor's back; he felt illicit as he grabbed his ass. And what an ass. Fox had gone on about it before in his head, but man, whatever Taylor was doing when he worked out, it was working out for his ass.

Taylor thrust his hips into Fox's groin while Fox urged him on with his grip. Taylor came back, braced over Fox on his elbows and held a condom and a bottle in front of his face.

"Lube," Taylor said, hips still moving. "You ever finger a girl?"

Fox nodded. He hadn't really been into it, but he liked watching the girl get into it.

"Same thing, but it's just opening up, not, you know."

"Getting you off?"

Taylor nodded. It was a normal enough conversation, except they were grinding into each other, holding back from kissing as their lips brushed while they spoke.

"Okay," Taylor said and rolled off and onto his side, one hand bringing Fox with him. He slid his thigh over Fox's hip, his hard dick sliding up the crease in Fox's thigh. Fox's dick was pressed into Taylor's abdomen.

Taylor grabbed Fox's hand and guided him to his ass. "Can you do it like this?"

Fox trailed his finger up and felt Taylor's hole. He brought his hand back to pull Taylor's thigh higher, then tried again. It was an awkward angle, but as soon as Taylor kissed him, a little desperately, Fox knew he'd make it work. He brought himself up onto his elbow so he was slightly over Taylor and had his hands free, their hips still pressed together, and squirted some lube onto his palm and wet his fingers. He moved his finger down and touched Taylor's hole. Taylor grunted, and Fox looked at his face as he pushed his finger in. Taylor had his eyes closed. Fox pushed in and pulled out, spreading the liquid around.

"Another one," Taylor said.

Fox brought his finger out and then pressed his middle finger alongside his index finger and pushed back in. It was tight, but the lube was loosening him up. Taylor was panting and rocking back, and Fox was so horny he could feel his dick rubbing up against Taylor's abs without any conscious thought. Fox looked at his fingers, sliding in and out and getting slick, and he thrust a bit harder. Taylor would need another one if Fox was gonna get in there. If he was even gonna last that long.

"Can I?"

"Yep." Taylor sounded strained.

Fox looked up at his face. His lips were parted and his eyes were still closed, and Fox watched, fascinated, as he pushed in with three fingers. Taylor's breath was punched out of him. He was panting, and Fox almost lost it when he felt Taylor shove back into his hand. Taylor pulled away and rolled onto his stomach before Fox could do that. He was forced to move back as Taylor came up on his hands and knees.

"You wanna do it like that?"

Taylor glanced at him over his shoulder through the fall of his dark hair.

"Easier for the first time," Taylor said.

Fox nodded. It felt impersonal.

Taylor came up onto his knees as Fox shuffled around behind him. He brought his hand up around Fox's nape and turned his head so he could take Fox's mouth. They were pressed together, chest to back, tongues sliding together, and Taylor's hand in his hair was yanking him close. Fox rolled his hips up, dick sliding against Taylor's crack, and brought his hand around to grab Taylor's straining erection.

Fox put an inch between their mouths and said, "Okay."

Taylor slid back down, his hips tilted. Fox got the condom on, lined up, and pushed in. The head of his dick breached Taylor's hole, and he groaned as he draped himself along Taylor's back, his fingers sliding between Taylor's on the mattress. The position gave him leverage to push all the way in. Taylor panted beneath him, his chest heaving in and out until Fox thought he might not be okay. Then Taylor tilted his head, kissed Fox's jaw where he could reach, and breathed, "Move."

Fox did. It was heaven. Tight and hot, an incredible pressure on his dick. But more than that, it was Taylor. Fox had never fucked someone he really liked. It was different. He felt Taylor grinding back into him and chased the rhythm, so it felt like no one was fucking anyone; they were fucking each other – a dirty, slow grind of bodies meeting and chasing. Taylor's gasps were muffled by Fox's mouth as he met his kisses. The creak of the bed, the slap of skin, and the slick glide of their sweat as they moved filled the room, and Fox felt his orgasm and almost wished it would stay away. He wanted to keep doing this. But Taylor felt it too and pushed back, and Fox shoved forward and came, his dick pressing in and in and in as he groaned. He recovered his breath, dick still half hard, Taylor rocking back into his groin.

Fox reached under him, grabbed Taylor's dick, and stroked it, rough and fast, as he whispered to him that he was "so beautiful. Fucking, so beautiful, man; wanna fuck you again, wanna keep fucking you," and Taylor came with a gasp, his come shooting over Fox's fingers and slicking the way as Fox pumped him through it.

Taylor stilled Fox's hand by gripping his fingers, dragging them up his chest, and using the hold to topple them onto their sides. Fox pulled out and ditched the condom but stayed close, plastered to Taylor's back.

"Good?" he asked.

Taylor laughed. He craned his head back and Fox met him. It was one of those nice kisses, hot but not going anywhere.

20

♥

FOX GOT HIS THE next morning. Taylor was all, "You don't have to," but Fox was like, "Fuck that, I want to." And he meant it. He was half asleep and probably more honest because his brain hadn't fully woken up, but the thought of Taylor railing him was making his morning wood strain until he was rutting up against Taylor's abs and begging him, "Come on, man, fucking fuck me already."

"Alright, alright," Taylor laughed down at him. He was braced above him on his hands, the morning sun lighting him up above Fox.

He got Fox lubed up on his back and Fox shoved into it, shameless, and when Taylor went to roll him over, Fox refused.

"Like this."

Taylor met his eyes and said, "Okay."

He put the condom on, pushed Fox's thigh against his chest, lined up, and pushed in. Fox gasped. It was uncomfortable, and Taylor stayed still. Fox panted. Taylor let Fox's leg fall so he was cradled between his hips. He brought his hand down and stroked Fox's erection and kissed him. He stayed where he was until Fox broke the kiss, panted for him to "keep going" and met Taylor as he pulled out and thrust back in. They found a rhythm like the night before, and Fox felt like they were fucking each other so hard it was like fighting, but at the same time, they were each seeking the other one's pleasure, pushing and grinding and finding an indescribable feeling in the other one's gasps and moans and half-spoken curses and declarations.

Fox came first with a shout against Taylor's mouth and Taylor groaned and fucked him hard, fucked him right into the mattress until he was tumbling over the edge with him, his hips rutting in and in and in, like Fox's had, the feeling of his come warm even through the condom.

After Taylor had rolled off him with, "Sorry, sorry," as Fox hissed, Taylor got rid of the condom and propped himself halfway up against the pillows, lit them both cigarettes and pulled Fox into the cradle between his legs, Fox resting against his chest.

Fox took a drag and said, "I don't know which one I like better."

Taylor took a drag around the breath he was still trying to catch and brushed the hair out of Fox's eyes. "You mean taking it or giving it."

"Yeah. You?"

Taylor ran his hand down and traced Fox's collar bones as he hummed.

"I think. I liked you fucking me, but I don't think I'd like it-like it, otherwise."

Fox nodded and then screwed his face up.

"What?" Taylor asked.

"I don't think I'd like the idea of anyone else fucking me or like, you know, fucking them."

Taylor smiled, the soft one. "Yeah?"

"Shut up."

Taylor laughed, it was deep and gravelly, still sleepy, and Fox wondered how long until they could do that again. He said as much.

Taylor reached for the ashtray on the bedside table and butted out his cigarette. He came back and took Fox's mouth in a kiss, then let

Fox up so he could crush his cigarette, and then tugged him back in. And Fox guessed that answered that question.

21

THE WEEKEND PASSED IN a blur of getting a four-wheeler and tearing down the beach, Sadie and Maggie racing to keep up, Fox wrapped tight against Taylor's back; fishing and abandoning fishing for blowjobs; eating charcoaled sausages in bread with salad; drinking beer, smoking joints; watching the sun rise on Monday morning, after watching it set on Sunday; and fucking. So much fucking. Taylor gave him a sheepish grin as they packed up and Fox returned it. Yeah.

"I don't wanna go back," Fox said as Taylor pulled back onto the highway.

He felt rumpled and rough like he always did after holidays when he was re-wearing clothes, using a different water pressure and sleeping in a different bed.

"Where do you wanna go?" Taylor asked as he accelerated and swerved out to check the oncoming traffic and then gunned it to overtake a road train.

It sounded like a genuine question. It always did with Taylor.

"I dunno," Fox replied and put his bare feet on the dash, lit a cigarette. He pushed his hair off his face and shoved his hat on to hold it back.

"C'mon, you musta thought about it?"

The truck was dust behind them and it was open road until the city. Fox took a drag and then handed it to Taylor. Taylor took it and leaned his arm out the window.

Fox thought about whether or not he'd thought about it. He followed his mind back over the last few years since finishing school – to not getting the grade in English to pass Year 12, to working at the pub as a dish pig, and then agreeing he'd help Kalum out for a few extra bucks selling gear. He didn't reckon he'd dreamed of much in those years, except the foolish and idle thought that maybe he could study.

But he remembered when he was a kid and this guy came out to the farm and talked about having a glass bottom boat. The image of a boat in the wheatbelt, three hours from the ocean and the closest you ever got to water was the Albany Doctor in the late afternoon, Fox thought this thing sounded like a fantasy.

"You can see into the ocean?"

"Right under your feet," the guy said.

Fox didn't know how this guy knew his dad or what he was doing there. But he never forgot about that boat and what he might see if he went out on one. Later he heard about the Maldives, about the coral, and he thought, shit, I'd like to see that.

"The Maldives," Fox said.

"The Maldives?"

"Yeah," Fox continued, nodding. "I wanna see the coral."

Taylor nodded, butted his cigarette out.

"How bout you?"

"Not as exciting as that. But, I've always wanted to do the whole Europe backpacking thing," Taylor said, smile rueful as he looked at Fox.

"Why don't you?"

"Well, Jimmy for one thing," Taylor said and slowed as they came up behind another road train. "And I got a debt."

A debt? Fox wanted to ask. But it felt private. His mum had a lot of debt. He didn't reckon it'd stop her pissing off to Europe if she felt like it. She once declared bankruptcy over a vacuum cleaner. He told Taylor as much.

Taylor laughed. "Yeah, not that kinda debt."

Fox huffed. "If you wanna tell me, tell me. If you don't, then don't."

Taylor gave him a surprised look, then returned his eyes to the road. "It's not telling you. Or, well, it is."

He reached for the cigarettes and Fox batted his hand away and grabbed them, lit one, and handed it over. Taylor took a big drag. Fox made himself sit quietly even though Taylor's answer hurt him in a way he couldn't explain.

"Not cos I don't trust you, I do, obviously," Taylor gave him an attempt at a filthy look, and yeah, Fox got that, but Taylor looked nervous too. Like he did before they fucked.

"I just, you know, don't want you to think I'm a piece of shit."

"I don't."

"You might, if you knew I let someone else take the rap for something I did. Let em go to prison for it."

"No way."

"Way."

"What'd you do?"

"Killed Tony's dad."

Fox was silenced. But then he couldn't help himself. "No fucking way."

Taylor snorted. "Way."

"When?"

Taylor glanced at him. "Most people would ask why."

Fox shrugged. "I figure he had it coming."

"You figure that, do you?"

Fox shrugged again.

"That I had a right to take his life cos he was a fucken asshole?"

"If he was a fucken asshole, then, yeah. Fuck him."

"Big words," Taylor said, but he said it in a way that sounded like someone else, like he'd been told that and was repeating it, not believing it.

Before Fox could reply, Taylor told him. Taylor was sixteen. Tony's dad was, in fact, an asshole. No surprise there. Nothing exciting, bit of a drunk, violent. Used to hit Taylor a lot. Said he was a pussy, a queer. Which, Taylor smirked at Fox, Taylor was. But, one day, Taylor decided to thump him back, only once he started, he couldn't stop. When Tony came in Taylor was sitting on the couch, Tony's dad was dead on the floor, and Taylor looked up, met Tony's eyes and said nothing. Tony's eyes had widened, but he was already into some heavy shit by then, so, he just said, "I'll take care of it. Get out of here."

Fox didn't understand why Tony would do that.

"Why?"

"Why'd he do it you mean?"

"Yeah."

Taylor rolled his shoulders back into the seat, one hand on the steering wheel, the other one tapping the window. "I reckon, back then, he wanted to protect me. He'd been inside already, reckon he thought I wouldn't make it."

Fox bit his tongue on the: sounds pretty fucking noble for Tony.

"But he also woulda seen it as a way to own me," Taylor finished.

And there it was.

"What a prick."

"Yeah," Taylor said. "I shoulda done the time. I woulda got three years as a juvie – murder downgraded to manslaughter for provocation. Tony got that and ended up doing seven on a fifteen-year sentence. But I was too young and I didn't think to, you know, argue with him."

"Uh, yeah, you were probably in shock, man."

"Probably."

"So, what's the debt. Like when you gonna be out of it?"

Taylor looked uncomfortable. "I sorta haven't paid it yet."

Fox frowned.

"It's joining."

Fox sucked in a breath.

"I know."

Taylor brought his other hand to the wheel and lifted his fingers, then wrapped them one by one on the wheel.

"Does anyone else know?"

Taylor glanced at him and then took his meaning. "Jimmy. Now you."

Fox raised an eyebrow, saw Taylor see it and huff a laugh.

"Yeah, I've thought about it, but it's harder to cover a murder than you might think. Plus, I don't wanna be that guy."

"Again," Fox said without thinking.

At least Taylor laughed. "Again."

Taylor exhaled long and then spoke like he'd been thinking the words for a long time and was finally getting them out, "I mean, sometimes I wonder if there's something wrong with me that I don't feel worse about it, you know? But then I think about animals, about an animal in a fight, always in a fight with a bigger one; like, I dunno, a lion or something. One day the smaller one's gonna be strong enough and if he gets the advantage he's gonna go in for the kill isn't he?"

Fox didn't think Taylor wanted an answer. It was rhetorical. It was also true.

"That's what I've always felt about it anyway."

"Makes sense," Fox said.

He needed to piss. He said as much.

Taylor gave him a quick look, like he was checking in.

"What?"

"You're not freaking out. Or like. You know what I mean," Taylor huffed as he scanned the side of the road for somewhere to stop.

"I know you," Fox said, easy.

"You do, eh?"

"You know what I mean," Fox shifted in his seat, looked at Taylor. "I mean unless you're playing me for a big 'fuck you, queer' at the end of this, which, that's a fucking long game right there."

"I'd never."

"Yeah, I know. I know you."

Taylor pulled to a stop where the gravel widened and a thicket of trees flanked the road.

Fox unclipped his seatbelt and Taylor gripped his wrist. Fox looked up. Taylor kissed him. Fox kissed back and would've kept going, gotten right into this!, but – "I gotta piss."

"Go, piss," Taylor said around a smile, his lips brushing Fox's. "Your fucken bladder, man."

"Fuck off." Fox got out and headed for a tree. The last road train they'd overtaken thundered past and honked his horn and Fox gave him the finger while he got his dick out.

22

F OX COULD SEE IT after that. Like his vision had been given a new filter. Tony acted like he had something over Taylor, and of course, he did. But that wasn't it. Or that wasn't all of it. There was an impatience about Tony with Taylor, but there was also a fear.

Not like Fox saw Tony much, Taylor did most of the pick-ups and drop-offs at the club so Fox wouldn't have to go there. Fox appreciated it. Taylor knew he did. Fox showed Taylor his appreciation with his mouth on Taylor's dick after Taylor had dropped him at his place and gone back out to the clubhouse to make the drop and then come all the way back again. Taylor reciprocated with drawn out fingering while his hand teased Fox's cock – "Edging," Taylor called it. Taylor would edge Fox until he was hard again and then he'd fuck him, face to face the way Fox liked, or chest to back on their knees, a deep, slow fuck that grew desperate and rough as they approached climax.

Point was, in between selling gear, fucking, and going on "dates" – "Yes, Fox, this is date," Taylor would say when he steered him into the old Italian place in Freo with a bottle of wine so they could eat their body weight in pasta and get drunk on BYO – Fox saw the whole thing in a new light.

"Tony's scared of you," Fox said into the darkness.

He was sprawled over Taylor's chest, tracing his finger down his skin, following his path with his lips, exploring but not leading anywhere. The street light lit up Taylor's profile with a streak of blue-white, Sepultura's *Roots* finished and tripped over into some mellower industrial stuff Fox didn't know, the sound drifting in from the living room. Taylor was smoking a cigarette and idly running his other hand up and down Fox's back.

"Yeah, probably. He doesn't like it, but."

Fox propped his hands on Taylor's chest and rested his head on them. Taylor brought the cigarette to Fox's lips and he took a drag.

Taylor gripped Fox by the nape with his other hand, his fingers a warm pressure.

"That makes him pretty dangerous," Taylor said.

Fox leaned into the touch, and Taylor loosened his grip and ran his hand up into Fox's hair.

"You ever thought about, I dunno, just bailing."

Taylor leaned away to butt out the cigarette.

"I had, yeah."

"Yeah?"

"Yeah."

"Europe?"

"Maybe. Jimmy's for a bit, probably. But he'd just tell me to go, give me the shits after a while."

"Yeah, but like," Fox kissed his pec, and then went on, "what's stopping you?"

Taylor huffed a laugh, squeezed Fox's neck. "Really?"

"Yeah, really," Fox said and kissed his other pec. Maybe Fox should start working out.

"Well, I kinda got this boyfriend here, and he's planning to study. So," Taylor trailed off.

Fox stopped, lifted his head. His heart thumped.

"Yeah?"

"Yeah, man. I mean, if you want?"

"No, yeah. I mean, yeah, I know. I already thought."

Taylor laughed, a soft huff of air. "You already thought I was your boyfriend? Presumptuous, babe."

"Fuck off. It's not like I'm fucking anyone else."

"Well, I hope not."

Fox wriggled and lowered his head so he could kiss Taylor's chest more. And hide his face, even though it was dark.

"And you?"

"Me what?"

Fox groaned. "Don't make me say it."

Taylor tipped Fox's face up with his fingers. Fox looked into his curious expression, his smile small and warm, and Fox said, "You're not, you know. Anyone else."

Taylor scoffed. "Fuck, no. After all the effort I've put into locking you down."

Fox grinned and ducked his head again. "Cool."

"Cool," Taylor agreed.

Fox's heart was going triple time and Taylor brought his hand around to Fox's chest and rested it there. It felt hot against his skin. He could feel Taylor looking at him, and he knew Taylor wanted to say something. But he rolled Fox over, pressed his body against Fox's and kissed him instead. And Fox thought maybe this was him, saying it.

23

I N THE DAYS THAT'D turned into weeks that'd turned into months that'd turned into it already being February and Fox being in a relationship – a real fucking couple, he couldn't believe it – but with all that, he'd kind of forgotten about days like this.

He'd come out of his room after spending the night at home for the first time that week – it was Thursday – and his mum was there, sitting at her usual spot at the little table, cigarette in hand, black coffee at her wrist, and a happy smile on her face when he walked out.

"Morning," she said.

"Hey," he replied. He felt the familiar mix of elation and dread seeing that look.

"What're you up to today?"

Fox had been planning to call Taylor and see if he wanted to go to Trigg, maybe even Lancelin, just driving and smoking and maybe stopping somewhere for the night.

"Not much," he said.

He turned the kettle on and reached up for a mug, his back to her.

"I thought we could go shopping." He heard her light another cigarette; she inhaled it loudly and then shot out the exhale on a harsh breath. She always smoked like that, noisily and angrily, like she was doing battle with the thing.

"What for?"

"Clothes? What else? If you're going to get a real job, you're going to need new clothes."

She drank her coffee. She did that loudly too – the liquid went down her throat with a gulping sound when she swallowed. It was Fox's own personal nails down a blackboard. He clenched his teeth.

"Hey," Austin said as he walked in.

Guy was like an apparition of hope, waltzing in at all the right moments.

"Hey," Fox said and poured the hot water.

"Fox and I are going shopping," their mum told Austin, "if you want to come."

Austin started laughing. It began like a chuckle and then he was heaving with it.

His mum frowned. She was pissed, Fox could see it, but she was working around it.

"You can just say no, Austin. And it's not like you couldn't do with some new clothes as well."

She butted out the cigarette.

"Clothes shopping, eh?" Austin grinned at Fox.

"Fuck off."

Austin laughed again as his mum said, "Language."

The phone rang, and Fox dived for it without thinking; he launched himself over the kitchen bench and knocked the table as he slid to his feet on the other side. His mum sat back, surprised and angry, but Fox was intent on the receiver, and he snatched it up and said, "Hello."

"Fox?"

"Hey," Fox said as he picked up the phone and the cord and lifted the whole thing over his mum's head and ignored her narrowed eyes as he tripped into the living room, shaking the cord out behind him.

"Hey," Taylor sounded like he was smiling. "What're you up to today?"

Austin brought Fox his coffee. Fox took it and nodded and said, "Thanks," and then to Taylor, "Gotta go shopping with my mum."

Austin started laughing again as he walked out.

"For real?"

Fox squeezed his eyes shut and cleared his throat in irritation. He knew his mum was listening, so he just said, "Yep."

"Damn, eh. I was hoping we could hang out," Taylor said.

And the thing was, Taylor wasn't a hugely emotive guy. Fox knew he, whatever, was fully into him, but he was still a guy. He sounded disappointed now though.

"Maybe later," Fox said.

"Yeah, but I've got that thing tomorrow."

And Fox remembered this now too. Taylor was going up north with Tony and the rest of those fuckwits for some club opening. Taylor was also paranoid about his phone.

Fox groaned and banged his head on the glass door.

Taylor huffed a laugh, but it was more of disappointment than amusement.

"I'll come down after, we can hang tonight?"

"Sounds good, but might not wanna stay," Taylor said. "Got an early pick up."

"Oh, yeah, course." Fox tried to hide his own disappointment.

Fox said he'd get the bus from Carousel and Taylor said he'd meet him at the pub there instead and Fox said he didn't have to do that, but Taylor said, "'S cool, see you then," and hung up.

Fox dropped the receiver down with a clatter and sighed.

The shopping trip was as excruciating as Fox expected. His mum was being super nice – pulling out clothes she knew he'd like; and she'd always been good like that, paying attention to shit – and that's what made it awful. The incongruousness of the whole dynamic. He didn't have Austin's clear-eyed hatred and capacity to define himself by never, ever forgiving the bullshit, no matter how nice she was afterwards. And he'd never have Clarissa's ability to manipulate the situation to her benefit. He was a stupid raw nerve to whichever mood was in play and his guilt over feeling hateful when she was a bitch was compounded when she was like this.

"Shall we get lunch?" she asked once she'd bought him new jeans, two new shirts, and a jumper.

Fox looked at his watch and shook his head. "I'm meeting a friend."

"Oh."

And that 'oh' was so fucking loaded, Fox didn't even want to look up. She could've interrogated him – she knew it was Taylor. She didn't.

She said, "Well, have fun then," and wandered off, a small figure amongst the other shoppers.

Fox sighed. Maximum guilt extracted. He turned the other way and headed for the pub.

Taylor was at the bar, a middy in front of him, some guy Fox didn't recognise sitting on his other side. Taylor was laughing at something the guy said. The guy grinned at him, his mouth still moving as he obviously told some hilarious story.

Fox suddenly felt ridiculous with his new clothes and his pathetic shopping trip with his mum and his job as a dish pig.

"Hey," he said as he reached Taylor's elbow.

Taylor twitched at his voice and then turned to him. His smile was warm and pleased as he said, "Hey, man."

Taylor looked back to the guy he'd been talking to and introduced them.

"Yeah, we've met," the guy said and shook Fox's hand. The guy's smile was sleazy, which was really unnecessary considering he winked as well.

Then Fox recognised him.

Taylor said, "We went to school together."

"I remember," Fox replied and nodded for a beer when the bartender came over.

"Shopping?" Cisco said. Only, he didn't say it like an insult, more like he was pretty curious about it, which he also proved by grabbing the bag and rifling through it. He hummed and commended the shirts, shook his head at the jeans and then gave the bag back.

"Ass like that? You want tight," Cisco told him.

Fox saw the bartender raise his eyebrows at Cisco as he set Fox's beer down. Taylor chuckled and shook his head.

"Cisco here was telling me about his band getting asked to play in Kalgoorlie," Taylor said to Fox.

Fox almost choked on his beer. Cisco was grinning.

"You're in a band?" he decided to go with.

"Sure am," Cisco said. "We normally stick to Connie's. Or, well, we only do Connie's. Then this guy who goes there says he's got a gig for us. I thought he was joking. Says he's not. So, the Exchange it is."

"You're gonna do it?"

"Why not?"

Cisco said it like a challenge. Fox was glad Taylor answered.

"Uh, cos you're gonna get pelted with beer cans if you do?"

"Pfft, won't be the first time," he shrugged, like he really did not give a flying fuck about a bunch of miners and bikers pitching beer cans at him and his, presumably, flaming queer band.

"What're you boys doing now anyway? Got any plans?" He drew the last word out, like plaaannss, and Fox went red. He sipped his beer to cover it. Cisco laughed. Taylor clapped Fox on the thigh. It looked platonic, like a friendly tap, but Fox saw Cisco see it and smirk.

"I dunno. I was gonna see what Fox wanted to do," Taylor said.

Fox wanted to go and hide somewhere and hopefully fuck Taylor wherever that place was.

"Maybe go to Freo?" he asked.

"Yeah?" Taylor replied.

"How romantic," Cisco said and rolled his eyes. "Well, I'm out. I've got a fitting for this show and then I'm meeting someone. We won't be going to Freo," he said and cackled.

Cisco finished his beer, slammed it onto the bar, his "Later boys," thrown over his shoulder as he walked out with another wink and sleazy up and down for Fox.

"He's not really gonna play the Exchange is he?"

"I think he really is, yeah," Taylor said and finished his beer too. Fox still had half. He shook his head.

"He'll be alright," Taylor said.

Fox took a gulp of beer. "He probably won't."

"Guy he's meeting? Franco, he's the bouncer at Connie's, he'll go with them."

It took Fox a second, but then he got it. "Oh. Still."

"You'd be surprised how many people don't really wanna fight once they know the person they're fighting can actually fight. Franco can fight," Taylor said.

Fox slid his beer to Taylor and Taylor smiled and took a drink.

"You really wanna go to Freo?"

"Not really," Fox said.

"Cool," Taylor shook his head when the bartender came over. He stood up and said, "You ready?"

Fox drained the glass, tipped it on its side and followed Taylor out.

24

♥

FOX WOKE SLOWLY TO the sound of banging. He shoved his face into Taylor's chest and mumbled for Taylor to make it go away.

"Oh, fuck," Taylor said and pushed Fox back.

Fox blinked his eyes open and moved out of the way as Taylor shuffled out from under him.

"Tony," Taylor said.

"Fuck."

There was no need to say it – they slept through the alarm. Or, Fox had a vague memory of it going off, and Taylor hitting it while mumbling about "Five more minutes" and then Fox was asleep again.

He was certainly waking up now as he watched Taylor vault over him and off the bed and grab for his boxers and jeans and toss Fox's to him. Fox caught them and threw the blanket off. He lay on his back and yanked them up his legs. He glanced at Taylor pulling his shirt on, and had a moment to feel like an absolute piece of shit – putting Taylor in this position – but then Taylor's head popped through the shirt and he gave Fox a quick grin and said, "Just stay here until we're gone okay?"

Fox nodded, his heart hammering. The pounding on the door started and stopped again and a voice that wasn't Tony's said, "Hurry the fuck up!"

Taylor grimaced. "Kevin."

Fox returned the look – Kevin was an insecure fuckwit of the highest order; he was also like, forty and yet he acted like he was eighteen, which made him a million times worse.

"You gotta be in a car with that for six hours?" Fox asked, keeping his voice low to mirror Taylor's.

"Ten," Taylor replied. He patted his pockets, looked satisfied, and then he leaned in, kissed Fox hard and fast. "See you when I get back?"

"Yeah course," Fox murmured against his lips.

"Taylor! Hurry the fuck up or I'm gonna leave your ass here!"

"I should be so lucky," Taylor said and kissed Fox again.

"Later," he said as he pulled away.

"Bye," Fox said.

Taylor pulled the door closed behind him, giving Fox a quick smile as it shut. Fox listened as Taylor's feet padded up the hallway, and then he heard the front door open.

"What the fuck time you call this?" Fox heard Kevin ask, his voice carrying from the entrance.

Fox couldn't make out Taylor's response, but then Kevin was off on a rant about how he wasn't taking his bike to babysit Taylor's stupid ass on the way there cos Taylor was a fucken pussy who wouldn't get a bike.

Fox listened, sitting up in bed, shirtless, and his anxiety gave way to rage. Taylor wasn't saying anything. Fox imagined him putting his boots on.

"I gotta piss," Kevin said and Fox heard his heavy footfalls coming his way, while Taylor was saying, "Not that door," and Fox flattened himself with the covers over his head and went completely still as he heard the door open, pause, and then close again.

Fox didn't think he was breathing. He heard Kevin go into the bathroom, piss, and come out again, saying, "You filthy dog. Gonna share?"

"Huh?" Taylor said, he sounded fucking pissed.

"You reckon I missed the chick hiding in your bed."

Fox didn't know whether to laugh or have a heart attack.

Taylor though, he didn't sound relieved, he sounded fucking mad. "Get the fuck out with that shit, you filthy fucking pervert. Get out. I'll meet you at the car."

"Woah! Keep your fucken pants on. Tony always said you were a tight ass, greedy little bitch," Kevin said, his voice fading as the front door was opened and then closed.

Fox stayed completely still. He couldn't hear Taylor moving either. The apartment was quiet, like it was holding its breath. Then Taylor's footsteps headed for the front door. Fox waited for it to open. It didn't. The steps came back, quickly, and the door opened.

"Fox?"

Fox poked his head out. He felt ridiculously ashamed.

"You okay?"

Fox nodded. "Course," but his voice cracked as he said it.

Taylor frowned, but all he said was, "Stay as long as you like. I'll be back Sunday."

"Kay."

Then Taylor gave him a filthy smile and Fox smiled back.

"You look good in my bed. Stay there."

Fox laughed, quiet.

"See ya," Taylor said and pulled the door closed.

Fox lay there for a long time. Taylor was probably in Lancelin by the time Fox felt unfrozen enough to sit up and get a cigarette.

He knew Taylor meant it, Fox could stay all weekend if he wanted. He left after that first cigarette, locking the door behind him.

25

F OX SPENT THE WEEKEND with Kalum and Hayley and some
of the hills crew. They got shitfaced and swam in Hayley's pool
during the day and at night Fox worked at the pub and then went
home; he was drained in that weird way he got when he drank all day,
then sobered up while working. It was good though. The normality of
it. The absence of that tension around Tony and those guys. It helped
dissipate the wired feeling he'd had since fleeing Taylor's place.

He got home from his shift on Sunday night and Clarissa and
Austin were sitting in the living room, watching a movie.

"Hey," he said as he came in.

"Hey," Austin said.

"What're you watching?" he asked as he swung himself onto the
couch.

But he could see it was *Silence of the Lambs*. Austin said it anyway.
Fox watched with them. He liked this bit, where Lecter asks Clarice
what the thing was, in and of itself.

"Taylor called," Clarissa said after a while.

Fox's heart thumped. "Did he want me to call back?"

"I dunno? Probably," she said, her eyes still on the TV.

Fox heaved himself up. "Where's Mum?"

"Work," Austin said. He was eating Twisties.

Fox mumbled that he was gonna use her phone and Clarissa said, "Like we care, just shut up."

"Fuck you," he said and went into his mum's room.

He dialled, watching the circle roll back with each number, quick circles on the first few digits, and then the long drag on the last four.

It rang. And rang. And rang out. Fox dropped the receiver back down and stayed where he was. Maybe Taylor went out. Fox didn't like that for some reason. Which was stupid – he didn't own Taylor and besides, it's not like Taylor was under any obligation to sit around waiting for his call.

The phone rang.

Fox picked it up.

"Hello?"

"Hey," Taylor's voice sounded scratchy. "Sorry, I was asleep."

"Fuck, sorry."

"Nah, it's all good. Was hoping you'd be here."

"Huh?"

"In my bed, where I left you."

Fox laughed. "Yeah?"

"Yeah. What're you up to?"

"Nothin, just got home."

"Work?"

"Yeah."

Taylor hummed.

"You sound tired."

"I'm fucked, yeah."

"Long drive?"

"Long fucken weekend, but yeah, that too."

Fox made a noise of agreement and then they breathed together for a bit. Taylor's breathing was going deep and even.

"Hey, go back to sleep."

"Hmm," Taylor said.

"I'll talk until you do," Fox felt kind of stupid suggesting it, but then Taylor said, "Yeah, please," and so Fox did. He told him about the weekend. He heard Taylor huff a sleepy laugh when he told him about Kalum passing out at Connie's last weekend and checking his ass like a lunatic when he woke up. He talked about how they were watching *Silence of the Lambs* and it always made him homesick for the farm. He talked until he said, "Taylor?" and heard nothing but breathing.

"Night, Taylor," he said and hung up.

26

♥

THAT FRIDAY, FOX WENT with Kalum to the clubhouse. Taylor had never said, "We can't rock up to that together," but, Fox knew they could not rock up to that together. Sometimes, Fox got the feeling Taylor wanted to say something about it when it came up. Fox always changed the subject. Taylor would get this look on his face, grateful yet resigned, and they never talked about it.

Fox still hated these fucking things, but at least he got to go back to Taylor's after.

Kalum picked him up after his shift and if Fox was dreading it, Kalum was next level. By the time they were turning onto the sideroad that'd take them the backway to the clubhouse, and Kalum had snapped about the music, about another driver pulling in front of him – pretty fucking legally, Fox thought – and hit his horn at a guy jogging past as the light changed, Fox was bewildered.

"Jesus, what's with you?"

"What? Nothing," Kalum jutted his chin at the jogger – who was giving them the finger – and then screamed out the window, "Yeah, you better fucken run!"

Fox bugged his eyes out at him, "Man, what, nothing? That dude could take us both."

"No, he couldn't."

Fox lit a cigarette as Kalum drove ten below the limit.

Fox exhaled. "Seriously, what's wrong?"

"Just, fucken," Kalum hit the steering wheel. "Hayley."

"What about her?"

"We had a fight. She doesn't want me going here anymore."

Fox took a drag and then said, tentative as he could, "But like, you don't really wanna go here either, right?"

"What the fuck, she can't tell me what to do!"

Fox's eyes bugged out again. Kalum was a super chill guy.

"Did she, but?"

Kalum deflated. "No, she just said, like, these guys are shit, and I was like, I know, babe, it's just money and she was all like, how much money do you need?"

Fox wanted to say, "sounds reasonable. It's not like your mum's filching your pay packet." Kalum's parents were really fucken nice. Sure, they barracked for Collingwood, but Fox could look past that.

He said nothing. Kalum parked. As far away as he could get.

Kalum sighed, he looked at Fox. "You're right. I don't wanna go."

"Then why do you then?"

Kalum looked at him, then away, a squirrelly look on his face.

Fox was pretty fucken curious now.

"Come on, man," Kalum said and waved his hand at the building. It was dark, but loud. "I'm not letting you go in there alone."

Fox was surprised. He shouldn't have been. But he was.

"I," he started and stopped.

"I know you got Taylor now," Kalum said and looked anywhere but at Fox, ran his hand through his hair. "But, you're still my best mate. I got your back, you know?"

"I know."

Kalum nodded. "Good." He undid his seatbelt.

Fox flicked the butt out the window and then reached over and gripped Kalum's bicep. Kalum looked up.

"Go home," Fox said.

Kalum shook his head. "What'd I just say?"

"No, I'm serious. I'm having one beer and then bailing with Taylor. Promise. Go home. Don't ever come back."

Fox watched Kalum war with it.

Then Kalum said, "Promise?" He winced at himself after, maybe he thought it sounded childish. Fox didn't care.

"Promise."

"And what about next time?" Kalum said, like a challenge.

"I reckon there won't be many more next times."

"Serious?"

"Yep."

Kalum exhaled loudly. "Yeah, okay. I don't like it, but."

"Yeah, me neither, but I like it better than you goin in there when you don't need to anymore."

Kalum nodded.

"Call me if you get stuck. I'll be at Hayley's."

"Cool," Fox said. "But I'll be alright."

He got out and waited while Kalum reversed and swung back around. Fox waved and Kalum gave him the finger and a grin and sped off. Fox laughed. He turned for the clubhouse, some awful base heavy shit was pumping out of it and for a moment he panicked at the thought of Taylor not being there yet. Then he thought how he'd look going in and gluing himself to Taylor like a little fag. He'd have to go up and get a beer first. He coughed, cleared his throat, and kept his head down as he marched inside and said, "Hey," to the ugly fucker on the door who ignored his greeting.

Fox made his way to the bar with his head still down, his eyes scanning the room as much as he could from the angle as he went. No one really paid him any attention and there was a space at the bar. Candy was on again and she came right over.

"Beer?"

"Yeah, thanks, thank you," he said.

She grinned at him, winked, then spun on her stilettos and bent over the bar fridge, her white G-string showing everything.

"Man, what I wouldn't give to get in there," came from his left and he looked up.

Kevin.

Eww, Fox thought, but he just gave a cough-grunt-nod in reply and then took the beer with a "Thank you," when she slid it over.

"And for you?" she asked Kevin.

"You know what I want, baby," Kevin replied.

Candy gave him a "Tsk, tsk," still smiling, and went for the bourbon.

"Not what I meant, sweetheart," Kevin said. It was a joke, but Fox could hear the edge in it. He bet Candy did too, but she just poured and slid the drink over and then Kevin pulled out a stack of two dollar coins and if Fox were Candy, he'd roll his eyes and groan, but she just smiled and indulged the old pervert, and Fox watched the whole thing and wished he was anywhere else. The problem with these things was that once you were in them, even this little bubble with Kevin, it was difficult to get out without an interrogation.

Fox chanced a look around the room – eyes tripping over black clad male bodies and half naked and naked women, his gaze moving too fast as they skimmed over Taylor, who was looking back. Fox backtracked quick and met his eyes. Taylor was near the wall and some guy Fox had seen but never spoken to was talking to him. Taylor brought his beer up – an imperceptible nod as he did so, his eyes never leaving Fox's – and sipped. Fox nodded, coughed, cleared his throat again and startled when Kevin hit him on the back.

"Jesus, you might wanna slow down on the smokes."

"Yeah," Fox said.

Candy was gone and Kevin was watching him. That wasn't good. So far, Fox had managed to stay off everyone's radar.

"You don't say much, do you, kid?"

"Um, guess not?"

Kevin nodded, like he approved, but then he said, "You been workin with Taylor, haven't ya?"

Fox swallowed, told himself to calm down and then nodded. "Yeah."

"How's that goin?"

There was something in Kevin's voice, that edge.

"Good?"

"Is that a question?"

"What? No?"

"Well is it good or isn't it?"

"It's good."

"Is it now?" Kevin said like he didn't want an answer. He was pinning Fox in place with his beady look. And fuck, he was ugly. He looked like he'd had real bad acne when he was younger, and then maybe he'd decided to work in the sun for twenty years and do too many drugs and drink and smoke too much and pour all that shit on top of those craters so he ended up looking like this. Old Leatherface.

Fox sipped his beer and didn't say anything.

"Ya reckon ya too good for us, kid?"

Kevin delivered this question in the most conversational way, but Fox did not miss the implications. At all.

He drew in a breath and met Kevin's eyes. "Whaddya mean?"

Kevin sized him up. He probably saw what Fox did – a fatter man measuring himself against a taller, yet to completely fill out one. Fox wondered for a second if Kevin might have a gun.

"I reckon you know what I mean."

"I never thought about it."

Kevin hummed like he knew it was a lie and was about to say something else when the sound of Taylor's voice greeting Candy was at Fox's back.

Fox turned like it was a polite and normal thing to greet your, whatever, workmate, and said, "Hey."

"Hey," Taylor said back, gruff, then nodded at Kevin.

Fox always felt a mix of fear and desire when he saw Taylor like this. Cold and closed off, dangerous.

"Whiskey or beer?" Candy asked.

"Beer'll do," Taylor said.

"You drinkin whiskey now?" Kevin asked.

"No," Taylor said.

Fox already felt like he was in the middle of something and they'd barely exchanged a few words. He sipped his beer and faced forward.

"Why'd she ask if you wanted whiskey then?"

Taylor accepted the beer, thanked Candy, and looked at Kevin. He looked like he wanted to murder him.

"Taylor doesn't mind some top-shelf every now and then," Candy said, smooth.

"Yeah? How would you know?" Kevin asked her.

"She works here," Taylor said like Kevin was fucking stupid.

"Is that what this is?" Kevin barked a laugh.

"Yeah, what'd you think it was?"

And Fox had never seen Taylor get into it before. He usually, as far as Fox had seen, said nothing. He wondered what the fuck had happened on that trip.

"Don't be a fucken moron," Kevin said. "You know what this shit is."

"Yeah, work. Some of us do it," Taylor retorted.

Kevin started laughing. It did not sound amused, at all.

"Oh, Taylor, you stupid fuck. So that's who was in your bed. Tony know?" Kevin shook his head. "What, ya reckon she likes you? Likes your fucken cash more like."

Fox saw the flash of surprise flicker over Taylor's face. He extinguished it with a swig of his beer and a short laugh.

Kevin's eyes darted to Taylor and Fox saw him realise he'd misread the play and he was losing ground.

"I gotta piss," Fox said.

Kevin jerked like he'd forgotten he was even there.

"Like we need to know that, fucken hell," he said, but Fox was clutching his beer and heading for the toilets at the rear of the warehouse before he said anything else. He pushed the door open and placed his beer on top of the paper towel dispenser and went for the urinal. He let out a deep breath and wondered if he could sneak out the window. He wanted to go home with Taylor – he hadn't seen him all week – but he was beginning to think he'd just like to get the fuck out of here more.

Fox pissed as quick as he could. He hated getting waylaid at the urinal even more than at the bar, and he thought maybe that was unfair. Some of the older guys were alright. In so far as they just nodded at him and ignored him. He was tucking himself away when he heard the door opening. He held his breath and hoped it was one of the old dudes.

It was Taylor.

He looked wound up, but he gave the stalls a quick once over and then turned to Fox, smiled, and said, "Hey," like a gust of air.

"Hey," Fox said and moved around for his beer. He could feel the heat of Taylor's body as he passed, aware of him at his back as he listened to him unbuttoning his pants and then pissing. Fox grabbed his beer and stood where he was. He waited while Taylor finished, listened to him washing his hands.

"You good?" Taylor asked from behind him.

"Can't wait to get the fuck out of here," Fox replied, low.

Taylor grunted, pulled out a hand towel at Fox's left, his body so close they were almost touching.

"Meet me at the car," Taylor said, right near Fox's ear, and then he went for the door. It whooshed open and the sound from the room rushed in, then dimmed as the door blew back and closed.

Fox took a deep breath and went out. He made his way to the bar, which was full now, but the spot where the girls came and went was empty so he went over there and drained his beer.

Candy saw him and spoke into the ear of another girl and she came over.

"Another one?" she asked. She had kind, terrified eyes.

"I'm good." Fox handed her the empty.

Someone hollered at her and she winced, hid it, said, "Okay," and went to take another order.

Fox turned his back on the room and headed for the exit at the opposite end of the bar from the one he came in. It was hardly ever used, and there was no one around. He pushed the door open and felt the cool summer night air hit him like relief. He sucked in a breath and heard footsteps behind him.

Fox glanced over his shoulder just as Taylor came up beside him.

"Parked at the back," Taylor said and fell into step with him.

Fox exhaled, coughed.

"You still got that?"

Fox hacked up some fluid, grunting as he swallowed around it. "Comes and goes."

"Kevin, that fucker," Taylor said.

"Huh?" Fox didn't get the segue.

"I saw him slapping you on the back."

The lights on Taylor's car blinked as he unlocked it, the beep-beep of the immobiliser a welcome sound against the boom of the clubhouse behind them.

"Oh, yeah."

"Fucker ever lays a hand on you again, I'll fucken kill him."

Taylor got in after he said it. Fox went to follow him when he heard Taylor's name. Taylor must've seen whoever it was, cos he got out.

"What," Taylor said.

The guy appeared out of the dark. He had a girl pressed against his side. The scared looking one from the bar. Well, she looked less scared now, but still not quite right. Fox recognised the guy in the same way he recognised most of these guys. As vague outlines – young, old; associate, nom, member; fucking dick, less of a dick. This one was young, member, less of a dick.

"Headin out," the guy said.

"What's it look like."

The guy raised his palms, "Alright, alright." He dropped his hands and tucked the girl into his side. "Later."

Taylor got in again and Fox followed. He started the car and peeled out of there like the place was on fire.

"You alright?" Fox asked.

Taylor lit a cigarette, handed it to Fox and then lit his own. They cruised past Carousel, made the turn for the highway and Taylor shook his head.

"Not really, no."

Fox didn't know what to say to that. He felt guilty. Which was stupid, what'd he done?

"It's not, like."

Taylor glanced at him.

"We're cool, right?"

Taylor gave him a surprised look. "Yeah, man. We're golden." He stopped at the lights and really looked at Fox. "Aren't we?"

"Yeah, I mean. I think so?"

Taylor clapped him on the thigh. "This's got nothing to do with you. You're the best thing I got goin on."

Fox blushed and shook his head with a laugh. "Fuck, I feel sorry for you then."

Taylor laughed. "Yeah, I mean. You could blow me more. But you know, whaddya gonna do?"

"Hey, fuck you, I blow you plenty."

Taylor hummed. "Cept for those lonely mornings when you're not there."

Taylor accelerated left onto the highway. "My dick misses you."

Fox laughed, smoked his cigarette.

"My dick misses you too."

Taylor grinned at him.

Fox finished his cigarette. "Why're you so pissed at them? I mean, more than usual."

Taylor butted out his cigarette, checked his blind spot and changed lanes.

"They just ridin my ass about joining, which means," Taylor took the exit that'd take them straight to Hammie Hill and then continued, "they're tryin to make me feel small until I do."

Fox squinted at Taylor's profile in the driver's seat. The way he smoothly shifted into the right lane and gunned it down the empty street. He couldn't imagine Taylor ever looking small.

"But you don't let them," Fox said.

Taylor glanced at him, then back at the road.

"I try not to."

They got a clear run and didn't say anything else.

Once they were inside Taylor's place, Taylor holding the door open for Fox and then following him in and kicking it shut, Fox was turning and kissing him. Taylor gave a start but then wrapped his arms around Fox and kissed him back. It felt urgent, volatile, and Fox felt himself pushing into it, asking for more.

Taylor broke the kiss, his hands coming up to cup Fox's face. "Yeah?"

"Yeah," Fox said and kissed him again before they could say anything else.

Taylor moved them into the apartment and down the hall, kisses desperate and breaking only to gasp or remove a shirt, their hands roaming.

Fox let Taylor topple him onto the bed and they fought with each other's pants, swearing and attacking until Taylor shoved Fox onto his back and Fox felt the breath whoosh out of him. Taylor got Fox's pants off, then his boots and then his own and they were finally naked. Fox pulled Taylor to him, bodies entwined as Fox chanted, "Come on, come on, come on."

Taylor fingered him open, Fox grinding into it, and then shoved a pillow under his hips, lined up and pushed in. Fox threw his head back and keened. Taylor kissed his bared throat, his lips wet and breath warm against Fox's skin. He fucked him deep and hard, his hand jerking Fox off with the same rhythm and it felt so good Fox thought he was gonna cry.

"Gonna come," he gasped.

Taylor kissed him and fucked him harder at the same time, his hand tightening on his dick until Fox came, his cries muffled in Taylor's mouth. He went limp as Taylor kept fucking him. Taylor went to pull out and Fox clamped his legs around his waist.

"Stay."

Taylor searched his expression, his hips still rocking. He groaned and buried his face in Fox's throat as he fucked in hard and fast, brutal. Fox panted and then he felt Taylor was gonna come before he did, felt it in his groin and chest before he felt it inside, felt Taylor pushing in as far as he could go and pulsing as he pushed further.

As they came down, Fox rubbed Taylor's sweaty back, kissed the top of his head, and held him close.

27

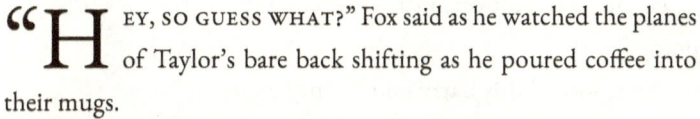

"**H**EY, SO GUESS WHAT?" Fox said as he watched the planes of Taylor's bare back shifting as he poured coffee into their mugs.

"What?" Taylor said with a smile over his shoulder. His hair was all mussed and hanging in his eyes.

"I got the weekend off."

Taylor brought the mugs over, his smile growing. "Have you now."

"Yep," Fox said and took the mug, blew on it.

"Got any plans?"

"Nope."

Taylor hummed as he came round the bench. Fox spun on his stool tracking the movement. Taylor came up between his legs, placing his mug beside Fox's elbow. Fox spread his legs wide to accommodate him and then enfolded Taylor between his thighs in a loose grip.

"Wanna go to Lancelin?" Taylor asked.

"Yep."

Taylor chuckled and took his mouth in a soft kiss.

"You're easy to please today."

"Nah," Fox said and leaned in for more.

There was a thump on the door and they both jerked back at the same time. Taylor met Fox's startled expression and frowned. Taylor hadn't moved back. Fox wondered how thick the curtains were.

"Yeah?" Taylor shouted.

"It's me," a deep voice said. He said it pretty softly, Fox thought. He watched as Taylor's frown turned to confusion and then an apologetic look, like he was embarrassed.

He extricated himself from Fox's thighs and went to the door. Fox spun around and reached for his cigarettes.

He heard Taylor open the door and say, "Barry? What're you doing here?"

"Hey, sorry," this Barry said. "Can I come in?"

"Why?"

Taylor didn't sound rude, more like he wasn't interested in letting the guy in.

"C'mon. What? Are you busy?"

Fox heard Taylor's hand brace on the door, but he didn't say anything.

"Ah, you're busy," this Barry said. "That was fast."

"What're you doing here, Baz?"

"You know what I'm doing here."

Now Fox was really fucking curious. He craned his head over the kitchen bench, and he could see the expanse of Taylor's body bracketing the doorway and beyond him, just a sliver of a big dude, maybe Taylor's size, surfie looking. He saw Fox before Fox could jerk back fast enough and Fox heard him chuckle.

"Nice," he said to Taylor.

Taylor didn't say anything, but the silence felt pretty damning this time.

This guy didn't seem deterred. "Well, give me a call when you're free."

"Yeah, that'll be never. Later."

And then the door slammed. The guy, Barry, laughed through the wood and then Fox listened as his footsteps thundered down the stairs.

"Sorry," Fox said.

"Christ, what for?" Taylor said as he came back in.

"Looking."

Taylor shrugged and grabbed his mug. He gave Fox a kiss, hard, and then took the cigarettes and went for the couch.

"Look all you want," he said. "I aint ashamed to have you here."

And well, they both knew that wasn't entirely true, for either of them. Nice thought though.

"Who was that?" Fox asked. He'd spun his chair so he was facing Taylor sprawled on the couch.

Taylor sighed. "Guy I used to fuck."

"No way."

Taylor looked uncomfortable. "Way."

Then it clicked.

"So he was here to..." he trailed off.

"Yep," Taylor said and focused on the smoke billowing out of his mouth.

"At ten in the morning?"

Taylor laughed. "Guess so."

"Wow."

Fox felt a few things about this. One, a booty call at ten on a Saturday? Fucken baller. Two, the guy was bigger, hotter, and older than Fox. Which led to three, he was kind of jealous? Shit. Yeah, he had an ugly feeling climbing its way up his chest, and it was probably gonna come out of his mouth.

"But you're not, with him?"

"No, course not," Taylor sounded affronted. Then he sighed. "C'mere."

Fox picked up his mug, padded over and slid onto the couch so he was pressed all along Taylor's side.

"It was just fucking."

Fox sipped his coffee and sat forward. He lit a cigarette, exhaled and said, "Doesn't make me feel better, man."

Taylor was quiet. Then he said, "Are you," he hesitated. "Are you jealous? Of that guy?"

"It's stupid."

Fox smoked his cigarette. Taylor sat forward too and gripped his thigh.

"Fox, we're like, together. That guy was a fuck."

"A recent fuck?"

And oh God. He sounded like a woman. He suddenly felt bad for judging all the women. He'd gone from happy morning after to fucken seriously bummed.

"Not since I met you."

Fox nodded. "I'm being stupid. I just, he's hot, man. And I'm," Fox shrugged.

"You're fucken perfect," Taylor said and Fox scoffed.

"Seriously," Taylor said. Then after a moment, "I kinda like it though."

Fox glanced at him, Taylor was smirking. Taylor brought his face closer until his head was resting on Fox's shoulder and he was draped over his back.

"What?"

"You. Jealous."

"Shut up. I don't. I feel like a little bitch."

"Nah, you love me," Taylor said and for once, Fox held his eyes when shit got all sappy.

"I do, you know," Fox said.

Taylor stopped smiling. Fox's heart plummeted. Even though all the evidence was there, he still couldn't believe it.

Taylor inhaled, his eyes never leaving Fox's. "I love you too."

Fox exhaled, shaky, and when Taylor kissed him, he was there for it.

28

THE DRIVE UP TO Lancelin was one of those perfect road trips. They had an esky on the back seat full of beer, snacks and cigarettes in shopping bags behind their seats, and some eighties shit that Fox had to admit after they'd pushed out of the city and the sprawling suburbs tapered off and gave way to the spindly bush between the city and Lancelin, was actually growing on him. The windows were down and Taylor had his elbow resting outside, cigarette in hand, hair flying in the wind, belting out Tears for Fears. Yeah, Fox thought, it was pretty fucken cool.

Before they went into the town proper, Taylor pulled off and drove to a clearing and told Fox they could camp here if he wanted. Fox had seen Taylor toss the swag in the back and figured they were gonna go to the caravan park.

"Fuck yeah," Fox said as he looked around. It was secluded, a patch of earth behind the dunes.

"Sweet," Taylor said. "Let's get a counter meal before we set up."

He reversed out and they went into Lancelin. The pub was quiet and Taylor spoke to the barmaid, who he seemed to know, and grabbed a couple of menus and two middies.

"How d'you know everyone?"

Fox slid into his seat opposite Taylor. The chairs were those shitty old plastic things, and Taylor kicked his back and raised his eyebrows. "Whaddya mean?"

Fox inclined his head at the barmaid. She was an older lady, like his mum's age. Taylor followed his gaze.

"Tanya? I wouldn't say I know her, know her. I've just been here a bit," Taylor said.

"Yeah?"

Fox had been here a bit too, mainly to surf. He never talked to anyone except Kalum and whoever else they came with. Taylor said he usually pulled off the highway to come through here whenever he was heading north. Got drunk, camped, got stoned, hung out.

"Who with?"

"Myself," Taylor said. "The steak sandwich is good."

"Okay." Fox told Taylor he'd get it and went up to the bar and ordered.

"Steak sandwich?" Tanya asked before he could order.

"Uh, yeah. Two," Fox said.

"He always gets the steak sandwich," she said with a smile. She was really small, with little glasses and nice clothes.

"Doesn't usually bring company though." She took the menus. "Beers alright?"

"Uh, yeah," Fox said and thought they'd just got them, of course they were.

"Be out in a few," she smiled again and disappeared into the kitchen.

Fox walked back over to where Taylor was supposed to be.

"Fox," Taylor's voice came from a dark corner on the other side of the bar.

Fox went over to him.

"*River Raid*," Taylor said.

He'd set up their beers, cigarettes, and an ashtray between them on the game.

"No fucken way," Fox said and took the other seat. "I used to play this game."

"Reckon everyone did," Taylor replied. And he didn't even need to ask, Fox was sitting down and kicking his ass in a matter of minutes.

Their food arrived and Fox said, "Better than poker."

Taylor laughed. "Maybe."

They ate. Drank more. Said bye to Tanya. Drove back to the clearing and set up. By the time they were smoking up and the sun was setting, Fox had a nice buzz going and he wished he could stay in this moment forever. Or at least, stretch it out. He said as much.

Taylor took the joint from him. "Yeah. Same."

Fox watched the darkness creep in and the stars come out.

"But you got school," Taylor said.

It felt like it came out of nowhere.

"Huh?"

"School. Starts soon right?"

They were still lying on top of the swag, using the backpack to prop their heads up to drink their beers and smoke cigarettes. Fox looked over at Taylor. He was looking up at the sky. They had a small fire going – because Taylor was one of those people who could just get a fire going – and his profile was cast in orange, bursts of yellow, and shadow.

"Oh, yeah. Dunno."

Taylor turned his head to face him. "When's the term start?"

Fox sighed. "Monday. But I'm probably not, you know."

"Why?"

"I dunno, it was stupid to think, you know."

Taylor frowned. He didn't seem mad, more like, confused. "It was stupid to think you could go back to school?"

"Yeah."

"Why?"

"Cos I'm fucken dumb, alright."

"Are you?"

"Yeah, man. I failed that shit once, just gonna happen again."

"Yeah, but," Taylor wasn't matching his anger, he just seemed thoughtful, "you were younger then and like. It sounds like, maybe living with your mum made it, I dunno, tough."

Fox deflated. Taylor wasn't wrong.

"Yeah, and nothin's changed," he said and then raced to change the subject. "What about you? What're you gonna do?"

Taylor looked away. Fox huffed a laugh and shoved him.

"What?" Taylor said, but he was smiling.

"Not so nice is it?"

"What?" Taylor feigned innocence. But he was still grinning.

"Getting interrogated about what the fuck you're doing with your life."

"I'll give you an interrogation," Taylor said and shoved him and then pulled him back and Fox laughed.

Taylor stayed where he was, kind of sprawled half over Fox now. He leaned over him and drank Fox's beer.

"What the fuck, get your own."

"Yours tastes better," Taylor said and smiled down at him.

Fox was defenceless in the face of that smile. Taylor's hair was catching the light and the dark strands turned auburn.

"I dunno what I'm gonna do yet," Taylor said. "But I got this feeling."

Taylor finished the beer and lay so he was stretched all along Fox's side, his elbow on the ground, head propped in his hand, looming over Fox. He brought his other hand over and stroked Fox's hair out of his face.

"I got this feeling like, I'm gonna do something."

He was watching Fox as he said it, like he was willing him to get it. Fox thought he did.

29

FOX CRASH LANDED BACK to reality on Sunday night when he got home and his mum was drunk and teary and she was on him as soon as he came in the door.

"After everything I've done for you, after everything!"

Fox felt like he'd walked on stage into a play that was halfway through. Only thing was, he'd walked into the middle of this performance before and he knew it didn't matter that someone forgot to tell him when the start was, he knew his part.

He tried to avoid her and make a beeline for his room. Sometimes, if she was the right side of drunk, he could make it. One time, she lunged for him and fell and he had to help her up but then she hit him. Now he knew if she was that drunk not to stop and instead take his chance to escape.

This time, she was on the wrong side of drunk. Not quite there yet.

"Where d'you think you're going? Get back here young man!"

Fox stopped, shouldered his bag higher and said, "What."

"'What,'" she mimicked. "Is that any way to talk to your *mother*?!" She emphasised mother like it had some mythical quality he'd certainly never fucken seen but in this moment, he better get on his knees and fucking worship it.

He shrugged. "I'm beat. I'm going to bed."

"Where have you been?"

"Nowhere."

"You've been somewhere. With Taylor," and she delivered Taylor's name with so much venom, it drew Fox up short.

He hesitated a second too long and she pounced.

"Taylor," she spat. "And what have you two been up to, hmm?"

"Nothin, hanging out," he was looking at his feet as he said it.

"Is that what you boys do? Hang out?"

Fox looked up and she was glaring at him. Whenever she looked at him like this, he didn't think what Austin did – she's a crazy bitch, ignore her – no, he thought she might kill him.

"Yes?"

She scoffed, lit a cigarette even though she already had one burning in the ashtray.

"Do you think I came down in the last shower?"

He didn't answer. He wished Austin or Clarissa were here. They weren't – he could feel it, he was alone in the house with her.

"If your nanna was alive," she said, quietly, like a warning.

Fox felt it like a blow.

"If she knew what you were. Disgusting," she spat.

Fox made his feet move. He heard her moving and he ran the few steps to get to his door. He went through and slammed it and her fingers got caught and she screamed and pulled them back. He had a second to think to help her but then shut it, quick, locked it. She was going absolutely fucking nuts on the other side – screaming, swearing, telling him she'd call the cops on him for assault.

Fox breathed. Told himself to just breathe. He glanced at his night stand and thought about the Canning College acceptance letter and started laughing.

He heard his mum's voice travelling towards the front of the house – she was screaming, "just look at what he's done to me!"

Fox wondered if she really would call the cops. He reckoned that'd be interesting. And he had to think that to stem the panic.

Then he heard Austin's voice. Thank Christ. Fox couldn't make out what he was saying, but he could hear her clear enough. She sounded more controlled, in that way she always was around Austin, but still furious.

"Where's Fox?" Austin was saying. He sounded bewildered and dismissive.

"That little faggot's hiding in his room!" She shrieked it for Fox's benefit, and he flinched.

"Would you calm down?" Austin said.

"After everything I've done, it's always this little black duck," she was saying and her voice was travelling away from his room again. He imagined her getting her cigarettes, gulping down her wine, Austin rolling his eyes.

Only Austin didn't. He shouted, "Oh for Christ's sake, would you give it a rest!"

Fox's eyes widened. There was a silence. And then she filled it, quiet and mean.

"You've been waiting for this."

"Waiting for what? For what? You think I sit around thinking about what you fucken do? Fucken, just leave Fox out of it."

"Who do you think pays for this house, huh? Your father?" She spat that too. "Your fucken father."

"Yeah, alright, whatever, have another drink and fuck off."

Fox swallowed. He imagined his mum doing the same. Their household functioned on unspoken tension. What held them together was the lack of open warfare. Austin might as well have just declared it.

Fox held his breath.

Then she was off, like an explosion.

"Get out! Get out of my fucking house, you ungrateful piece of shit!"

Fox heard a light rap on his door. He knew it was Austin and he opened it and ushered him in. He heard her footsteps thundering towards them and he slammed the door. Locked it.

"Fucken crazy bitch," Austin said.

She was pounding on the door. Fox turned to look at Austin. He looked a bit wound up, but he was smiling. Their mum kept on screaming.

"So, ah, school tomorrow?" Austin said.

Fox started laughing. He covered his mouth to muffle the sound, but it was out there.

"She'll fuck off soon!" Austin yelled at the banging on the door and then sat down in the desk chair. He pushed his hair off his face and let out a whoosh of breath.

Their mum started saying she was going to call the cops and moved away from the door.

"Shit, man," Fox said.

Austin shrugged. "Let her."

"Not that, where're you gonna go?"

"Oh, yeah, I been meaning to talk to you bout that. I got a place, share house, but it's near the uni. There's another room, if you want?"

Their mum's footsteps came back and she said, "They're on their way."

"Good!" Austin shouted.

"I'll give you good!"

"That doesn't even make any sense," Austin said to Fox.

Her footsteps went away again and Fox sighed.

"Uni?" he decided to start with as he sat down on the bed.

"Yeah, I got in."

"Yeah?"

"Yeah, course," Austin said and rocked back in the chair. "So, you wanna get out of here?"

"Yeah, but. Clarissa," Fox said.

Austin scoffed. "She can handle herself. And if you stay here the pair of them are just gonna hock all your stuff," he looked at the floor as he said it. Fox's PlayStation was missing.

"Motherfucker!"

"Yeah. They bought smokes and booze."

Austin smirked. Fox was fuming, but he had to crack up.

"Yeah, alright. Just," he didn't know how to finish that sentence. He felt bad. For his mum. For leaving her.

"Gotta get out, man," Austin said.

Fox sighed.

"Yeah, I know."

They waited until they heard nothing for a while and then Austin told him he was moving out tomorrow, that he better go pack.

"Jeff's pickin me up at seven if you wanna come down then," he said as he went out.

Fox looked around his room after Austin left. The house was still. It felt like what he imagined those towns felt like after a cyclone. Only, in this house cyclones weren't seasonal.

He pulled down his big backpack and started shoving shit into it.

"**N**EDLANDS," FOX SAID INTO the phone in his new place.

Taylor whistled. "Nice."

"Nah, it's pretty shit actually, but it's near the uni and I can get the bus and like," he exhaled and looked out at the little yard. It was overgrown with weeds and the brick fence was buckling in. The sun was shining and lighting up the greenery, a golden halo on the edges.

"And like?" Taylor prompted after a minute of Fox saying nothing.

"Like, you know, you could come round? Stay, if you want. There's five of us, but everyone's cool," Fox finished.

"Yeah, sounds good," Taylor said. He sounded distracted though.

"Or we could just like, stick to yours."

"I wanna see your place," Taylor said and then sighed. "Sorry, I gotta do some drops."

"Oh, you want me to come?"

"Not really."

Fox's stomach dropped. Oh.

"I don't want you doin this shit anymore."

Fox frowned.

"Not really for you to decide, man," Fox said.

"Yeah, I know, but," Taylor sighed again. "Look, I gotta do this, talk later, yeah?"

"Yeah, course. You goin to the clubhouse now?"

"Yeah, I'll get this done and call you."

"Okay."

They said goodbye and Fox stayed where he was. Something didn't feel right. Eva came in and asked if he wanted a cuppa. Fox shook his head and thanked her again for letting him have the room.

She scoffed at him. "You're paying for it, it's all good," she said and took her coffee and went back to her room.

Fox had to get his shit ready and head into school the next day, explain why he was starting two days late. Austin said they wouldn't give a shit. He had the books, not the latest editions, but how different could Biology and Chemistry really get. Austin said the best thing about doing it this way was only having to take the two subjects and you got your score from that. Fox knew all this and should've been thinking about all this. He wasn't.

He went into his room, looked at all his shit still packed on the bed and the floor, and pulled his boots on. He grabbed his smokes and his wallet, and went to Austin's open door.

"I'm heading out for a bit," he said.

Austin was reclining on his bed, reading a book. "Kay."

Fox hesitated. Austin looked up from his book.

"I'm gonna go see Taylor," he said.

"Kay. Cool," Austin replied.

"Yeah."

Fox nodded but still didn't move. Austin put his book down.

"You know it's cool, right?"

"Yeah, I know."

Fox blew out a breath and ran a hand through his hair. "I'm just, dunno, worried."

Austin gave him a quizzical look, like he was trying to figure out what Fox was saying, and also how he was supposed to respond.

"Not about you guys," Fox said.

Austin nodded. "About Taylor?"

"Yeah."

"Dude looks like he can handle himself."

"Yeah."

"Is he like," Austin paused. "Joining that gang or whatever," he was smirking. Fox knew Austin couldn't quite get past the joke of it all. Who joins a fucking gang? he'd say, laughing.

Fox cracked a smile. "They want him to."

"And he wants to?" Austin asked like his whole opinion of Taylor hung on the answer.

"No. But it's, you know, complicated."

"It's never complicated," Austin said and leaned back further against his headboard. "There's shit you wanna do and shit you don't. Do what you want, don't do shit you don't."

Fox huffed a laugh. "Yeah, I guess."

"Seriously, man. You're not doing shit for them anymore right? I mean, you don't need to."

Fox shrugged. "Hadn't thought about it yet, but yeah, nah. Probably not."

"Cool."

"Alright, well, I'll be back later."

Austin nodded. "Later."

Fox caught the bus into the city and then walked to the train station and jumped on the train just as the doors were closing. It was hot when he got off and he had to walk a few kilometres to get to the clubhouse.

He'd probably miss Taylor given the time. But something made him keep walking.

By the time he turned onto the street, he was parched and he kept telling himself this was a stupid fucking idea and he should just go back. But his feet weren't listening and he kept moving forward.

The clubhouse came into sight and Taylor's car was parked out front. Fox's heart rate picked up and he kept going. No one was outside. Fox sucked in a breath to steady himself as he pushed the door open.

It was dark after the blinding sun and he couldn't see anything, but he heard voices stop and then, "Fox?"

Fox blinked a few times and Taylor came into focus. He was at the bar, Tony next to him. They had beers and it looked like a congenial conversation had been taking place before Fox walked in. He imagined what he must look like – sweaty, young, stupid.

"Hey," he said. He hadn't planned anything further than get here.

"Hey," Taylor replied. He sounded like he wanted to sound gruff, but it came off worried.

Fox saw Tony glance at Taylor and then at Fox and his expression didn't change but something that looked like understanding passed over his face.

"I'll be out in a sec," Taylor said. "Wait at the car." And that was cold. But Fox knew it was put on for Tony's benefit. He knew then that Tony knew it too.

Fox nodded and went back out. His heart was pounding. Fuck, fuck, fuck.

Fox lit a cigarette and heard the door whoosh open and clang shut behind him. Taylor's footsteps were approaching and Fox was too scared to turn around. The car unlocked with that familiar sound and Fox watched Taylor go past him and open his door. Taylor didn't meet his eyes as he pulled the door open and Fox made himself move and get in.

Taylor peeled out like normal, neither of them saying anything. The tyres crunched on the loose bitumen and Taylor turned onto the main road and the tread went smooth.

"Fuck, sorry," Fox said at the same time as Taylor said, "Tony knows."

Fox sucked in a breath. Taylor glanced at him, and then he reached over and gripped Fox's thigh, hard.

"I'm not ashamed."

Fox shook his head. "Fuck, I'm such an idiot. I thought, fuck. I thought you were in trouble. And I came, and now I've gone and fucked it all up."

Taylor tightened his grip and said, "No."

He took his hand back and exhaled roughly. "He was waiting for something."

Fox smoked his cigarette and asked the question he didn't want an answer to, "What's he gonna do?"

Taylor clenched the steering wheel.

"I dunno."

"We can't go back there."

Taylor shot him a pained look.

"I have to," he said.

"No you don't."

Taylor shook his head. "Even all that shit aside, I got this run. I'm not gonna do a runner. Then I'll have the whole lotta them after me. I'm not looking over my shoulder for the rest of my life."

"So, just like, drop it at the door and then take off."

Taylor laughed. It was edgy, but it broke the tension in the car. "That'd be pretty funny."

Taylor sighed and spun the car onto the highway. "Nah, I'll make the drop and then that'll be the end of it."

"Yeah?" Fox said.

"Yeah," Taylor nodded. "What're they gonna do? Force me to join?"

Fox didn't know. He said nothing. He especially didn't say that he was more worried about Taylor getting gay bashed.

"Are you alright?" Taylor asked after a while.

"Yeah? I mean, I just got you in a world of shit, so I feel like a fucken asshole, but I'm alright."

Taylor shook his head, he indicated and made the turn with a quick glance. "Nah, I was already in a world of shit, you just improved the view."

Fox snorted.

"But, seriously, you looked sick when you came in."

Fox sighed. "I was worried, it's stupid."

"Worried about me?"

"Yeah, Austin agreed it was stupid."

Taylor huffed a small laugh; his eyes crinkled as he glanced at Fox.

"Well, he didn't say that, he said you could handle yourself."

Taylor nodded. "I can. Nice though."

"What is?"

Taylor focused on the road and sounded uncharacteristically vulnerable when he said, "To have someone give a shit."

"Well, I give a shit."

"Thanks," Taylor smiled.

"So, what's the plan? I got school tomorrow, so if we could get this done, get you out and get to dick sucking before then, that'd be awesome."

Taylor shot him a grin and told him the plan. Six drops. Prearranged like always. Take their cut and then drop the rest. It was Tuesday, so the clubhouse should be pretty empty when they got there, which was ideal cos Taylor didn't want a scene or an audience when he told Tony he was finished. Fox insisted he'd be coming with him. Taylor didn't like it, but he said Fox could wait in the car. Fox said that made him feel like a kid.

"It'd make it easier. For me," Taylor said.

"Okay," Fox acquiesced and focused on the refinery whipping by.

"Sorry, but if you're there, then I'm gonna be worried about you."

Fox looked at him, at his hands resting easy on the steering wheel, on the wind whipping his hair around his face, his expression steady and focused on the road and he got it then. Taylor had found his resolve and he had to cross the Rubicon on his own. Fox still didn't like it, and he knew Caesar had an army behind him when he did it, but he got it.

"I get it. It's cool."

Taylor blew out a breath. "Thanks."

"Not a problem," Fox lit a cigarette as they slowed for the lights.

"Yeah, but," Taylor reached for the cigarettes and Fox handed him his and lit another one. Taylor smoked and said, "Thank you, for you know, everything."

Fox frowned and looked over; he didn't know what to say, or how to explain what Taylor's words made him feel. But he felt like he should be the one saying thanks, for you know, everything.

31

T HE SUN HAD BEEN set for hours and the clubhouse was dark and quiet when they got back. There were no cars or bikes, except for Tony's. Taylor blew out a breath.

"Thank fuck," he said.

Fox startled. He was jumpy anyway.

"You thought he'd call for backup?"

Taylor nodded. "Maybe."

"Jesus, mighta told me."

Taylor leaned down to Fox's feet and grabbed the bag. "You wait here."

"Yeah, man, I know the plan."

Taylor sat up but stayed in Fox's space.

"No matter what. You wait here," Taylor said and kissed Fox hard.

Taylor was opening his door and getting out before Fox could ask no matter what, what? What did Taylor think was gonna happen?

Fox watched him walk up the expanse of concrete, a dark figure against the washed out blue of the moonlight on the asphalt. Taylor belted the door open with his fist and it swung back, spilling light onto the pavement, and he went in, swallowed up by the light as the door closed behind him.

Fox sat back in his seat. He went for a cigarette and then sat back again. He'd smoked too much today. He hoped Taylor would make this quick. He bit his thumb nail until the nail split down the side and he was picking at the broken bit until it was bleeding. He was thinking he either need to rip it off or leave it when he heard a sound like firecrackers and his heart leapt into his throat. He heard Taylor shout something but couldn't make out the words. Fox's heart was going too fast and his breathing was too quick. He opened the glovebox and the gun was there. He grabbed it and jumped out. He wasn't thinking. He was jogging up to the door, gun in hand. He'd never held a gun, but you've seen the movies! He screamed in his head and he took a deep breath and kicked the door open and walked in.

"Fox, no!"

Fox had a split second to see Taylor standing, palms up near the bar before Tony was turning and pointing his gun on Fox. Fox lifted Taylor's gun.

"And here's your little faggot of a boyfriend," Tony said.

Fox's hand was shaking, but then he felt something in him steady, like the fear galloped through him and snapped, and on the other side was a wide open plain of calm.

Fox could see then that Tony had his gun trained on Fox's head. Right between the eyes. Fox knew he had his in the exact same position. All he had to do was pull the trigger.

"Dad was right about you, Taylor," Tony said but his eyes never left Fox's.

Fox could see it then too, like the future had skipped forward and he saw what Tony was about to do. When he would make the shot. And he was gonna make the shot. Fox knew it then like he knew the sun would rise. Fox's breathing was loud in his ears and he heard Taylor's voice but not the words.

"Filthy fucken faggots," Tony said and Fox fired.

Tony's head kicked back, but then he fell forward. It must've happened fast, but it felt slow.

Taylor was at his side and Fox turned to him, dazed.

"He was gonna kill you," Fox said. He sounded calm. He didn't sound like himself.

"I know," Taylor said. "And you gotta get out of here now, Fox."

Fox shook his head and looked at Tony on the floor. He was face down. There was blood pooling around his head.

"He was gonna fucking kill you!" Fox felt the surge of anger like power.

Taylor gripped his shoulders and spun him to face him. Fox saw Taylor's eyes intent on his.

"I know," Taylor said again. "You gotta go."

Taylor slid his hand down, opened Fox's palm and pressed his keys into his hand.

"Can you drive?"

"Yeah, I got my license," Fox said.

Taylor huffed. "Fox, you're in shock. Can you drive?"

"Course."

"Good. Go."

"Where?"

"Home."

"What about you?"

"I'm gonna take care of this."

Fox didn't like that, he shook his head. "You come with me."

Taylor shook him. "Fox, I need you to do this for me. Go. Now."

Fox met his eyes again; Taylor looked upset. It broke through something in Fox. He leaned forward and kissed him, hard like Taylor had kissed him before in the car, and pulled back.

"You'll come to me after," Fox said.

Taylor looked pained, but he nodded. Fox clenched the keys in his grip and nodded back.

Fox handed Taylor the gun and turned to go. Taylor gripped his wrist and squeezed. Fox looked down at his big palm wrapped around his fairer skin.

"Thank you," Taylor said.

Fox looked up and met his eyes, he wanted to say so much but he had no words. He nodded again. Taylor let him go and Fox walked out. The night air was cool and his mind was blank. He got in the driver's seat. He turned the key and the Valiant roared. He reversed and drove.

32

Fox drove to Nedlands on autopilot. He turned onto his new street. The first thought he had was, I can't fucken parallel park, and then it hit him. What happened. What he'd done. What the fuck Taylor was doing. He almost threw it in reverse and gunned it back, but then he thought about Taylor's face. Fox shook his head hard as if to dislodge the pained look there. Taylor was back there, cleaning up Fox's mess.

And now Fox was idling in the street in Taylor's car. He saw a space on the verge under a tree and drove under it and parked.

As he got out, an old lady with a little white dog said, "You can't park there."

"Fucken tow it," Fox said.

She gasped and hurried on.

Fox didn't know why he said that. He wasn't that guy.

"Sorry!" he shouted down the street. And then he saw Tony's head – flicking back, the split second of realisation in his eyes – and Fox shook his head again. He rubbed his eyes and ran inside.

"Hey," Eva said.

"Is Austin here?"

"In his room. Are you alright?"

"I'm good, I'm good," he rushed out and ran down the hallway.

Fox busted through Austin's door. "I killed someone!"

Austin lifted both eyebrows.

"You fucken what?" a female voice said from behind him.

Fox turned and saw Clarissa. Thank, Christ. She was sitting in the desk chair, a drink in hand, expression unimpressed.

"I fucken killed someone!"

"What, like, accidently?" Austin said.

"Maybe don't yell about it," Clarissa said and sipped her drink.

They didn't believe him. He shut the door and started pacing. Then he told them what happened.

"Fucken, for real?" Austin said when Fox finished.

"Yes, for real!"

Austin whistled. "Shit."

"Fucken hell, Fox," Clarissa said.

"What am I gonna do?"

"Shower," Clarissa said.

"What?"

"Gun residue. Fuck, you guys watch more TV than I do, don't you know that?"

"I think he meant more, in the bigger sense," Austin said.

"Isn't Taylor taking care of it?"

"I feel like you're not taking it seriously," he said to her. "I killed someone."

"But he was gonna kill you or Taylor, probably both of you," Clarissa said.

Fox nodded. Then his head kept on moving.

"Here," Clarissa handed him her drink.

He drank it.

"I'll get another one," she said and went out.

"What am I gonna do?"

Austin's face transformed then. He got that cold look he'd gotten with their mum sometimes.

"Nothing. You do nothing."

"Whaddyamean?"

"I mean, nothing. Go to school. Carry on. Maybe avoid Taylor for a bit."

"I've got his car."

Austin sat back. He looked thoughtful.

Clarissa came back in. She handed Fox a drink. He took it and drank. She sat down and took a sip and Austin said, "You feel like going to Dad's?"

Clarissa turned to look at him. "When?"

"Now."

Clarissa looked between them. Austin said, "Gotta hide a car."

She shrugged. "Yeah, alright."

Austin shuffled forward and reached for his boots.

"Wait, wait," Fox said.

"You gotta move that car."

"But, Taylor," Fox said.

"He can handle himself," Austin said again. "You keep that car here and you're gonna get interrogated and Fox? You'd suck at that."

"You would," Clarissa drained her drink and stood.

"Okay, just."

"Shower, quick," she said and flicked her hand at the hallway.

Fox nodded. He got himself into the shower and then he felt the tremors. He rushed as he lathered up and rinsed off, trying to steady the shaking. He towelled off and went to his room and rummaged for fresh clothes and came into the living area where Austin and Clarissa were chatting with Eva like everything was fucking normal. He felt like he was gonna crack up. Austin gave him a look and told Eva they'd be back in a few days. Fox followed him and then paused.

"Eva?"

She hummed. "Yeah?"

"If Taylor, that's my um, my boyfriend, if he comes round, can you tell him," Fox blew out a breath. "Just tell him I've gone to see my dad and I'll be back in a few days."

"Okay," she said, but she was looking at him strange. He didn't reckon it was the boyfriend bit – he'd met her girlfriend – it was him.

"Tell him. Tell him I'll call him."

"Okay, Romeo," Clarissa said and grabbed him in a headlock to drag him out. She had to reach up to do it, but she was surprisingly strong. Or maybe he was just feeling weak.

"Jesus Christ, Fox," she said once they were on the street, Austin was ahead of them with the keys in hand. "Could you be any more pathetic?"

"What? What if he comes here and thinks I've bailed on him?"

She shoved him, not hard, more like a friendly hip tap.

"Not that," she shook her head, then mimicked, "Tell him, tell him I'll call him," only she did it in a really high-pitched, simpering voice.

"You do know I just killed someone, right?"

He meant, be a bit fucking nicer to me, not that he was planning to kill her.

She clearly got it, cos she said, "Eh, guy was a fuckhead."

"He was," Austin said as he got in the driver's seat.

"Should we call Dad?" Clarissa asked as she buckled her seatbelt.

"Nah," Austin said. "He'll be stoked."

And the thing was, Fox thought, he really would.

33

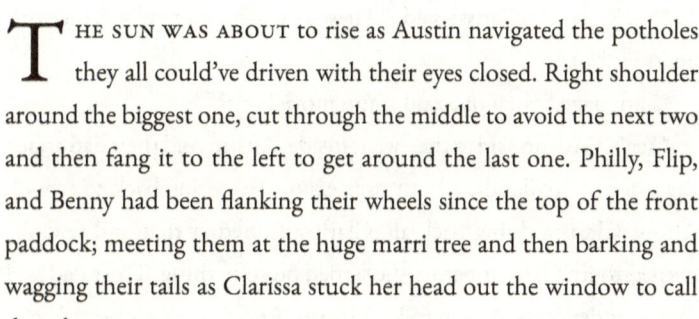

THE SUN WAS ABOUT to rise as Austin navigated the potholes they all could've driven with their eyes closed. Right shoulder around the biggest one, cut through the middle to avoid the next two and then fang it to the left to get around the last one. Philly, Flip, and Benny had been flanking their wheels since the top of the front paddock; meeting them at the huge marri tree and then barking and wagging their tails as Clarissa stuck her head out the window to call them home.

Austin pulled back to centre and drove up to the wattle tree. Their dad was there, a curious expression on his face and then he saw it was them and he grinned. Austin put it in park and they all got out.

"Austin," their dad said, his voice bursting with a quiet joy, "Clarissa, Fox."

"Hi, Dad," Clarissa said. "Fox killed someone."

Their dad laughed, grabbed her ponytail and shook it.

Austin rolled his eyes. "Thought we'd visit."

"Oh, great," their dad said, like they weren't actually there, but he was still super excited at the prospect. "Yeah, that's great."

"I need to leave this car here for a while," Fox said.

Their dad looked at the car. "Okay."

"Maybe up at the shed."

"Sure, you kids want some coffee?"

"Yeah," Austin said.

Flip jumped up on Fox's thighs, her little paws coming up to his knees and he picked her up and gave her the biggest cuddle. She grinned at him, tongue hanging out.

"So, how is your wonderful mother?" their dad asked as they followed him down the dirt path to the back veranda.

Clarissa laughed, Austin snort-laughed, and Fox cuddled Flip and tried not to laugh.

"She's good," Clarissa said. "These two assholes have left me with her now, but."

"Language," their dad said. "You moved out?"

"Yeah," Austin said as they went inside. Austin told their dad about the place in Nedlands. About uni. About Fox going back to school. About Clarissa doing fuck all. Clarissa huffed at that and said she needed to find herself before she settled on something. Their dad said that sounded wise. Austin rolled his eyes. And Fox felt cocooned here. He was home.

Fox drove the car up the little hill and put it at the rear of the shed, undercover, in front of the sheep pens. His dad came with him. As they got out, his dad surveyed the car and its position.

"It'll be alright here. There's been no rain, but just in case," he said.

Fox nodded.

"It's a very nice car," his dad said.

Fox nodded again.

"It's my boyfriend's," he said after a minute of them admiring the stationary vehicle.

His dad glanced at him, his expression unchanged; but then a slight smirk broke through, the one that said he was uncomfortable with his children trying to have an emotional conversation with him, but he was here for them nonetheless.

"Well, he has very good taste in cars," his dad finally said.

Fox looked at the car and not his dad. He thought about Taylor, doing God knows what with Tony's body, about how this was the second time he'd been subjected to this shit. He thought about Taylor's soft smile, just for Fox, and he thought about how he'd do anything for him.

"I need to leave it here for a while," Fox said.

"Leave it as long as you like," his dad replied. "Might need to turn the engine over every now and then, if you want to leave me the keys."

Fox handed them over. His dad took them and put them in his pocket. Fox stepped back and scuffed his feet in the dirt. The galahs were blanketing the back driveway – Fox couldn't see them, but he could hear them – screeching and feeding. The sun would be breaking over that rise now, a golden light that pierced over the little hill and lit them up like a sea of pink and grey feathers feeding on the wheat that spilled from the truck as it hit the same bump every time.

"Thanks, Dad," Fox said.

His dad huffed a laugh and ruffled his hair with his big palm. Fox might've shot up, but he'd never be as tall as his dad.

"Go on in and get some sleep. I'll head into town and get you kids some food."

Flip came trotting in then and launched herself at Fox when she saw him there – like she was realising all over again that he was here, he was really here – and he caught her up, pressed his face into her ratty fur and trudged back down to the house.

34

F OX HAD BEEN SITTING on his dad's bed for a long time trying to decide which number to call. His dad said of course he could use the phone in here. He could hear him and Clarissa and Austin through the wall, eating dinner and drinking and talking and he couldn't decide which number to call. He couldn't call Taylor's.

He dialed the Nedlands number.

"Hello?"

"Eva?"

"Krystal, is this Fox?"

"Yeah, hey, sorry, you guys sound the same."

"It's cool, we get that. Hey, some guy was here for you?"

"Taylor?"

"Yeah, that was him."

"When?"

"Last night, pretty late."

"What'd you say? What'd he say?"

"Oh, I didn't see him, Eva did. But she said he said to tell you he'd see you round."

Fox sucked in a sharp breath.

"That's all he said?"

"That's all he said, I think? Hang on."

Fox heard her calling for Eva, and then Eva must've come in because she was asking her and then the phone was being handed over.

"Fox?"

"Yeah, it's me."

"Fox, hey, yeah, your boyfriend was here and I told him what you said and that you'd call and you're at your dad's."

"And what'd he say?"

"He said to tell you he'd see you round," Eva said.

"That's all? How did, how did he," he trailed off, his eyes fixed on the soft pink bedspread his dad still had from when his mum lived here.

"Umm," Eva paused, like she was thinking. "He seemed tired, I think? And, I dunno, maybe sad you weren't here."

Fox squeezed his eyes shut.

"But then he was just like, 'well tell him I'll see him round' and he left."

"Fuck, okay. Thanks."

"Yeah, no problem. Hope it works out."

"What does?"

Eva seemed surprised by the question. "You and your boyfriend."

And what did that mean?

"Oh, yeah, thanks. We're cool."

"Oh, okay. Well, see you when you get back."

"Okay, bye."

"Bye."

Fox hung up. 'I'll see him round.' Fox reckoned he was just trying to be vague. Surely he would understand where and why Fox had gone – wouldn't he? Fox went back out and tried to join the conversation, but he kept playing the image of Taylor coming to find him and him not being there over and over in his mind.

35

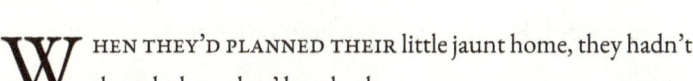

WHEN THEY'D PLANNED THEIR little jaunt home, they hadn't thought how they'd get back.

"Bus?" Clarissa said, but then their dad said Mrs McGlynn was going to the city on Friday if they wanted a lift. They did.

Fox was anxious the whole way, biting his thumb nail and trying to answer Mrs McGlynn's questions about school. Thankfully, Clarissa could keep a conversation going with a rock and so Fox was mainly left to stare out the window and think.

She dropped them back at the Nedlands house, saying it was no bother, even though her daughter lived on the other side of the river.

"What's an extra ten k after five hundred?" Austin said when Fox said she was really nice for doing that for them.

Fox guessed so. He followed Austin inside and was immediately accosted by Eva.

"Fox, your boyfriend's on TV."

"What?"

"Yeah, haven't you seen the news? Cops are looking for him," she said. She sounded excited.

Fox watched the TV as she turned it up. Their dad didn't have an aerial, and apparently they'd missed the news of a gang related execution and the search for a – not a suspect, Fox thought as he heard them say Taylor's name – person with information.

Fox sank into the couch, eyes glued to a mug shot of Taylor. It was an old picture. Taylor was maybe Fox's age in it. He tuned out the voices around him, and he knew one thing right then – Taylor wasn't turning up any time soon.

"Tell him I'll see him round," he'd said.

"Why do they want to see Taylor?" Eva asked.

"It's his cousin," Fox said.

"Your boyfriend's cousins with the head of a bikie gang?"

Fox nodded. He felt irritated to hear Taylor phrased like that, reduced.

"Well, they can't find him," Eva said.

"You didn't tell anyone anything did you?"

"What? No," Eva shook her head.

"Good. It's just, Taylor's not into that shit," he waved his hand at the TV.

"No, he seemed nice," she sat down in the armchair as she said it. "That's why I couldn't believe when I saw him there."

Fox was a bit stuck on the 'he seemed nice'; he was more than that, and now Fox was gonna have his work cut out for him trying to find him.

The phone rang and Austin answered it with a "ello?"

"Fox," Austin said.

Fox turned and Austin was holding the receiver out. His expression was blank, but carefully blank. Fox got up and took the receiver.

"Hello?"

"Fox," Taylor said.

Fox stopped himself from saying Taylor's name and where are you? How can I get to you? Are you okay?

"Hey," he said gruffly to hide the relief.

"Hey," Taylor replied.

They both said nothing for a minute, then Taylor said, "You alright?"

"I think I should be asking you that."

Fox turned his back on the room and looked out into the courtyard. He could see himself reflected back in the glass.

Taylor made a sound, like a huff of breath, and Fox could hear what sounded like a road train in the background, roaring past.

"You've gone," he said.

"For now," Taylor said.

Fox dropped his head and felt his eyes burn. He'd known. He hadn't wanted to know.

He sucked in a breath, it sounded wet.

"Hey now," Taylor said, his voice was gentle.

Fox shook his head and tried to make his voice work. He couldn't. He wanted to say so much – come back, take me with you, don't leave me, I love you.

"Hey, Fox, you gotta listen to me, okay?"

Fox nodded, managed to croak, "Yeah?"

"I gotta go away for a while, but I love you, okay?"

Fox nodded again.

"And you gotta go to school."

Fox huffed a wet breath, fuck, who cared about school?

"None of this was your fault, alright?"

Fox shook his head. That was bullshit.

"I gotta go," Taylor said.

"Please don't," Fox said and he heard how pathetic he sounded and he also knew he couldn't ask that. He did anyway.

"Fox," Taylor said, a breath of air, and then, "Take good care of my car," and then the line went dead.

Fox held the phone to his ear, listened to the dial tone. He watched the sunlight in the little courtyard shift; a willy wagtail was chattering and dancing on the wall.

36

THE MORNING AFTER HIS twenty-first, Fox woke in his bed on the farm and thought about Taylor. It'd been nine months since he'd seen him, and he was still his first and last thought every day. His dad had told him he got new plates for his car when he'd arrived a few days ago for his party. He'd walked up to the shed – the car facing out now instead of in – and seen the new plates.

"Thought maybe you could drive it now," his dad said.

Fox had looked over at him. He'd never really understood what his dad did and didn't know. He came off pretty naïve about city life in general, and if his mum was to be believed, he was a lazy good for nothing who did fuck all except read and occasionally sow a crop.

His mum was bitter and full of shit, but she was right about one thing – his dad did read a lot. Novels. News. History. Interviews. Articles.

He wasn't fucking stupid, he knew Fox was hiding this car for a reason.

"Maybe go find your boyfriend?" his dad said.

Fox twitched. Okay, reading was one thing, but insight was quite another.

He watched his dad shove his hands in his pockets and rock back on his heels.

"Clarissa told me about it," his dad answered his unspoken question.

Fox glanced up at him. He was looking at the car, not giving anything away with his expression.

"I don't know where he is," Fox said after a while.

His dad looked at him, his expression thoughtful. "Somebody does."

Fox nodded. "Jimmy maybe."

"So, go and ask him." His dad clapped him on the shoulder, gave it a good shake. "Then you can start uni."

Fox scoffed and shook his head. He still couldn't believe he'd got in.

Now he was waking up and thinking about what his dad said. "Maybe go find your boyfriend." He kicked off the blanket and grabbed his jeans, yanked them on and started mapping out the drive in his head.

After the police had arrested Kevin and laid charges for Tony's murder, Fox thought Taylor'd show up again. He hadn't. Fox also wondered how in the fuck Taylor had framed Kevin and wished he could've seen Kevin's face when the police arrested him.

But that was all beside the point now. Taylor hadn't reappeared. Kevin was waiting for his trial. No one had come knocking on Fox's door. The code of silence remained intact, which was about the only good thing Fox could say for those fuckers.

He got a coffee to go, the house still and quiet, and jogged up to the shed with the dogs. Taylor's car was where he'd left it, facing out, ready to go. Fox clicked the immobiliser and it beep-beeped at him – the sound as familiar as Taylor's huff of breath against his ear.

"Okay," he said to the dogs, "I gotta go, but I'll be back."

He gave them all pats, and Flip an extra one, and got in the driver's seat and started it. The car roared to life and Fox saw the fuel gauge was full. He eased out of the shed and around the back driveway, and the pink and greys flapped up in a shriek of noise and wings as he crept past them. He rolled past the house and saw his dad step out of his study onto the front veranda.

Fox lifted his hand off the steering wheel in acknowledgement and his dad smiled and waved.

37

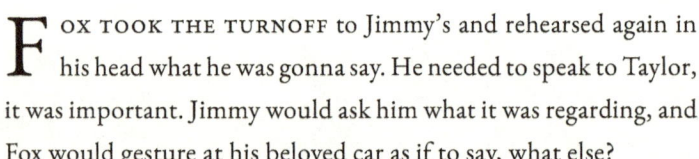

Fox took the turnoff to Jimmy's and rehearsed again in his head what he was gonna say. He needed to speak to Taylor, it was important. Jimmy would ask him what it was regarding, and Fox would gesture at his beloved car as if to say, what else?

Okay, it was a pretty fucking shit plan, but in the six hours it'd taken to drive here, he hadn't come up with anything better. He got out and did the gate, drove through, got out and closed the gate, got back in, and told himself to chill the fuck out.

Fox drove up slowly so he got a nice view of Jimmy hobbling onto his porch with his gun lifted, barrel pointed right at the driver's side.

Fox told himself not to panic. He'd prepared for this. If preparing was chuckling and telling himself that no way was Jimmy gonna pull his gun on him was preparing. He stopped. Turned the car off.

Jimmy didn't say anything.

Fox opened his door and stepped out, hands lifted.

Jimmy squinted at him.

"Was wonderin when you'd turn up," he said. He didn't drop the gun.

"I'm looking for Taylor."

"Well you aint lookin for me are ya? Course you're lookin for Taylor."

Fox still had his hands up. He felt ridiculous, but he couldn't bring himself to drop them just yet.

Jimmy didn't seem inclined to say much more.

"Do you know where he is?"

"Yep."

Fox felt a rush at the knowledge. He'd known Jimmy might, but to have it confirmed.

"Can you tell me?"

"Nope."

And with that, Jimmy lowered the gun. Fox dropped his hands but stayed where he was. He didn't know what to say; he wasn't Taylor, he didn't have that chill or ability to just know what to say, what to do.

But then, he reckoned he knew one thing. Taylor would want to see him.

"Taylor won't mind," he tried.

Jimmy spat and rested his arm on the gun. "Won't he now."

Fox was gonna continue, but Jimmy beat him to it.

"I know what you are. I know what the pair of you are. Coupla fudge packers."

Fox didn't know how to respond to that, so he just blushed and stood his ground.

"Yeah, that's right, ya reckon I don't know my own grandson?"

"No," Fox tried.

"No, I don't know him?"

"No, you do."

"Damn right, I know my boy. Never bothered me," he said like he was being really magnanimous. "Cos he's still a man, my Taylor. Not like that piece of shit Tony. Fucken Tony."

Jimmy shook his head with disgust, but then he grinned. "But he sure got it, didn't he?"

"Uh, yeah," Fox said and glanced at the paddock. There were some goats in it. He hadn't noticed them last time.

"Yeah," Jimmy agreed and Fox could hear him still smiling.

"What about you?"

Fox looked back at him. Jimmy was staring at him like a challenge.

"What about me?"

"You a man, kid?"

"Umm, yeah?"

"Well are you or not? Aint gonna have no boy with my Taylor."

"Yes, I think," Fox coughed, cleared his throat. "Yeah. I'm a man."

Jimmy laughed. "Yeah, you are. Fucken Tony," he said again and cackled.

Then he sobered. "I'm gonna tell you where Taylor is, you wanna know why?"

Fox steadied his excitement and asked, "Why?"

"Cos I reckon he's been waitin for you to come ask me. And I reckon I'd make you sweat cos you took your sweet ass fucken time about it."

Fox opened his mouth to object but Jimmy told him to, "Shut it," and then proceeded to give him the address.

Fox pulled out the map as soon as he was safely on the other side of Jimmy's gate. Jimmy reckoned there were roadworks on the Great Northern, said he'd better take the Goldfields route. Fox wondered how in the fuck old dudes always seemed to know what was going on with the roads, and then he saw it was gonna add at least a hundred kilometres to the drive. He was gonna need fuel. A lot of fuel. He blew out a breath and gunned it back to the highway.

38

FOX HAD BEEN SO excited when he tore down the highway, city giving way to farms and open stretches of land as he headed east, he'd reckoned he'd drive straight through. But by the time he got to Southern Cross, he decided to rethink that plan and stop in Kalgoorlie for the night. Not in the town proper – fuck, no; Cisco might be game enough to do a flaming queer show there, and Fox knew he wasn't exactly flying the flag like Cisco did with the way he looked, but Kalgoorlie wasn't a place you wanted to be gay and capable of shooting a bikie point-blank in the head.

Fox had come to realise a few things about himself over the nine months since it'd happened. And one of them was that he was, in fact, capable of killing. If he had to. He didn't want to have to. The other two things in this order, were: he was gay. One hundred percent. Not bi, not maybe eighty-twenty, but totally into dick; and he was head over heels, balls deep, in love with Taylor. No other guy was gonna cut it. He'd looked. Not gonna happen.

So he rolled into Kalgoorlie late that same night after he'd been to Jimmy's, after he'd driven from the farm to the city for the first half of the day, and he felt the fatigue overtake the adrenaline. He pulled into a little servo down the road from the Exchange. A guy came out to fill it up and Fox asked him about places to camp. The guy scratched his chin as he stood with the fuel pump in the car and said there were a few patches people camped in outside the town proper. "Not too far," he said.

Fox thanked him, asked him to get him some Twisties and a coffee and a hot chicken hero, paid him, and drove the fuck out of Kalgoorlie.

He found a spot. A patch of red earth surrounded by green bushes and no one around. Fox rolled out Taylor's swag and lay back under the black sky dotted with a million stars. He ate his roll and thought there was no way he was gonna sleep with the nerves skittering up and down his arms and the butterflies in his stomach.

Fox woke and it was still dark, but there was a cool blue on the horizon and he got up. He drank the cold coffee and thought about Taylor. He packed his shit quick and got back on the road.

It was five and a half hours to get to Wiluna and Fox only stopped in Leonora to get fuel, coffee, another hot chicken hero, and wash his face in a shitty bathroom.

He slowed as he drove through Wiluna and then accelerated once he was on the other side. His heart was pounding. Jimmy had said to go past the cemetery, said there'd be a dirt track on the right, follow the track and he'd find Taylor. Fox was hoping for a road sign, found none, but then there was a track. It had to be it. Had to.

He turned right and navigated the road, his eyes straining ahead of him against the glare of the midday sun to search the emptiness for a sign of Taylor's camp.

The light from the sun blistering above him hit something shiny and reflected back to him. Fox drove straight for it, heart hammering. The red dirt was a cloud around him and he knew the engine would be a roar in the deafening silence of the desert. So he wasn't surprised to see Taylor stepping out the little door of a caravan, strolling casual as you like in the red dirt and then stopping with his hand shielding his eyes from the sun as he watched Fox drive up.

Fox stopped, his eyes taking Taylor in. Fox killed the engine and got out; his body was stiff and his nerves and excitement were overwhelming. But the nerves were beat back when Taylor dropped his hand and smiled at him.

"You brought my car back," Taylor said.

"Yeah," Fox said on a breath, it felt surreal. "Thought you might need it."

Now he was here, he didn't know what to do. He was drinking Taylor in – the realness of him – his hair was longer and he was tanner, and he sure as fuck looked buffer. Fox had finally filled out more, but he felt inadequate in his shitty jeans and he probably looked filthy; but Taylor was still smiling at him, smiling like Fox was the best thing he'd ever seen.

"'M glad," Taylor said.

Fox shrugged. "You're welcome."

Taylor's smile widened, showing teeth, and Fox huffed a laugh and rushed him. Taylor caught him up in an embrace that crushed the air from Fox's lungs. He could feel Taylor's face pressing into his neck, feel his breath warm on his skin, felt more than heard Taylor whisper, "Fuck, I've missed you."

Fox gripped him tighter. "Me too, me too," he said into Taylor's skin.

They held each other and breathed for Fox didn't know how long. It felt good, better than that, it felt like coming home.

"Jimmy?" Taylor said after a while.

"Yeah," Fox was nodding against Taylor's throat. "Sorry I took so long."

Taylor pulled back, his face inches from Fox's and said, "You had school."

Fox huffed, "Fuck school. If I'd known."

Taylor shook his head. He slipped his hand around the back of Fox's neck and wrapped his fingers one by one on Fox's nape. Fox sank into it while his eyes searched Taylor's looking back at him.

"Fuck, I missed you," Fox said and leaned in to kiss him.

Taylor met him and kissed him back, a hard press of lips that shifted to the desperate kisses Fox remembered.

Taylor broke the kiss and rested his forehead against Fox's; he was panting and Fox knew him, he knew Taylor wanted to say something. Fox breathed, leaned in for another kiss, a brush of lips, and waited until Taylor murmured against his mouth, "How long?"

Fox understood.

"Uni starts end of February."

Taylor's eyes were shut, and Fox watched as his lips moved into a smile. "Four months?"

Fox nodded. "If you'll have me."

Taylor opened his eyes and smirked. "I'll have you."

Fox huffed, but he was smiling like a fool, and so he kissed Taylor again and broke away just long enough to say, "Bed."

"Bed," Taylor agreed and hustled Fox the few steps to his caravan, his hands roving under Fox's shirt and his lips on the back of Fox's neck. And as Fox stepped inside the unlit space, Taylor pressed up against him, an anchor in the darkness until Fox's eyes adjusted to the dim light.

Acknowledgments

Thank you to KP for being my cherished first reader and for proofing and consulting on later drafts. Thanks as well to my brothers, my other first readers – your feedback was entertaining and most appreciated. Big thanks to my dad for his readiness to talk about all things writing at all times. And thank you to my ex for helping with some details. And finally, thanks to my birds – there is no better writing companion than a bird. One galah in particular forced me to sit with her every day lest she feel flockless; I wrote this while chirping back and forth with her and fending off her random attacks, and thus, all mistakes that remain are probably her fault.

About Author

Sasha Avice is the author of nine novels (and counting!) and one PhD (which is enough). She lives with a changing cast of birds and a dog. When she's not writing or teaching, she's fostering birds. She loves hearing from readers! Email direct at sasha@sashaavice.com or join her mailing list at sashaavice.com for regular updates.

Also By

Perimeter
Series

"Out there on the perimeter, he ain't interested in love... but goddamn if it don't keep on finding him."

Set in Western Australia at the turn of the millennium, each book is a standalone featuring guys who don't want love, don't seek it.

They drift, they work... and then some guy turns up and the dull isolation goes bright, blinds them like a splinter of sun caught in the eye.

Shop now at Amazon.com for current books and future releases in this series.

Contested Possession
Series

"... possession is achieved as a result of winning a contest." *Australian rules football.*

Each book features a football player whose possession of the guy he wants is... contested.

Shop now at Amazon.com for current books and future releases in this series.